Martin J. Brown is a secondary school English teacher and Hall of Fame track and field coach. He has spent his life working with and for children in need as a counselor, teacher, and coach. He is a father of seven successful children and fourteen grandchildren. His writings have appeared in the op-ed pages of *The New York Times, The Wall St. Journal, The Bellingham Herald* and *Newsday*. He is the author of the riveting 2018 novel, *Chuckanut Dreams*.

Dedicated to:

#womanlifefreedom

Ryan and Ella,
One day I hope to walk freely with you on the soil of your ancestors

Martin J. Brown

No Borders for Truth

AUSTIN MACAULEY PUBLISHERS®
LONDON * CAMBRIDGE * NEW YORK * SHARJAH

Ordering Information
Quantity sales: Special discounts are available on quantity purchases by corporations, associations, and others. For details, contact the publisher at the address below.

Publisher's Cataloging-in-Publication data
Brown, Martin J.
No Borders for Truth

ISBN 9798891557482 (Paperback)
ISBN 9798891557505 (ePub e-book)
ISBN 9798891557499 (Audiobook)

Library of Congress Control Number: 2024918650

www.austinmacauley.com/us

First Published 2024
Austin Macauley Publishers LLC®
40 Wall Street, 33rd Floor, Suite 3302
New York, NY 10005
USA

mail-usa@austinmacauley.com
+1 (646) 5125767

2024/12/17

Acknowledgements

Firestone Library at Princeton University

Maryam Naghaviha

Patrick Riley

Deborah Schlein, PhD.,
Princeton University

Table of Contents

Chapter 1
Northern Tehran, Iran, Mid-1970s

"Mossadegh was gorgeous," Father rambled on once again as we sat at the dinner table, eating Mother's sumptuous array of vegetables, dates, and, tonight, lamb.

"He was our nation's greatest leader, as Uncle Jalal, who worked in the Iranian oil fields, told us. 'The Indians had their Gandhi, the Americans had their Abraham Lincoln, we had Mohammed Mossadegh...he was the angel who came upon us'."

"Where is he?" My bright younger sister, Esteri, would ask. "The imperialist British and their American lackeys, they..." With the singer Elaheh's music softly playing from a cassette tape in the adjoining parlor, Mother chimed, "Hamid, enough. Must we be treated to another political lecture?" Her penetrating chestnut eyes effectively forced Father, always to an obsequious nod.

Hamid, we have the Shah, you have a good job, and things are good. "Why must you ramble and subject our daughters to this nonsense?"

"No, please, Father, go on. I love sharing your thoughts," my older sister, Mahin, blurted out; *Clearly,* I thought, *the apple of my father's eye.*

"Shideh and Esteri," Father, setting his eyes on us, "for your sakes, I will ramble no further, your mother's right; Shah is good, we have the Golha, we have food on the table, we have each other. I will speak no more to politics."

"Insha'Allah," my sister Esteri murmured. This was a typical evening in our north Tehran home.

We were teenagers in the seventies, and our world was safe, or so it seemed, centered on education and living a devout Muslim life. We could pluck oranges from our orange grove in our tiny yard, as well as eat the cherries that fell from our neighbor's tree. The scent of a nearby eucalyptus tree accented the freshness of our lives. Mother idolized the queen, Empress Farah, and at least three of the rooms in our house adorned with pictures of her.

It was not until later that my sisters and I took notice that we were without a picture of the queen's husband, King Reza Pahlavi, *The Shah,* in our spacious home. As a strong mother to young women, it was a tacit understanding that we were modern, and now with the king and queen's reforms in place, the world was ours.

Mahin, the oldest of us, was ready to accept a scholarship to an American university in California. Two years younger than her, I was content to continue my studies at the University of Tehran, and my sister, Esteri, two years younger than I. She was the artist, with her father already having her painted picture of the nearby Alborz Mountains hanging in the center hall. Father was a mathematics teacher at the nearby secondary school, and his hero was the great ancient Persian mathematician Muhammed Al-Karaji, who, as a father would tell to whomever would listen, 'The world would not have the understanding of algebra, and water engineering without Al-Karaji'. Father had a cherished set of books on Al-Karaji's life locked in our center hall hutch. He was also always ready and able to quote the great Persian poet and mathematician Omar Khayyam.

With his notorious chuckle, he would often quote his favorite *Khayymism* at will. Mother was a student of Father at Razavi University. A forbidden question, and never told the story, was how exactly Mother and Father started their courtship while teacher and student. Father was an avowed Communist, and Mother was a hijab-wearing devout Muslim. Mother prayed five times daily, and Father did not. Once at a Nowruz family gathering, Mahin asked the obvious question. Father made it clear there would be a short and accepted answer, as both the relatives and we, grew silent in anticipation of perhaps a humor-filled anecdote.

In a terse tone, Father waxed philosophically, "Omar Khayyam told us, 'When you have planted the rose of love into your heart, your life has not been in vain'. Your mother planted that rose; that is all we need to know." My Mother and Father were so loving and accepting of each other, and each other's differences, and accepted Iran as it was, was a great contradiction of not only their life but the life we knew growing up.

There were forces that preyed on those differences, however. My mother's brother, Uncle Masood, a devoted Shah hater, would often quote an Imam who, at the time, we only knew as the 'voice of the Islamic Renaissance', according to Uncle. Father had yet to come home one night before Ramadan, and my uncle brought over a cassette tape and played for us the angry words of this man, who ripped apart the Shah, and 'the wretched destiny of the puppet of the Great Satan'. When Father came home, his eyes widening, the lines in his forehead straining, he asked Uncle Masood to step into the center parlor. He took out the cassette, and never again would we hear the voice of Ruhollah Khomeini in our home. Father explained, "Girls, that is the voice of hatred, and all that does is divide our precious land."

Mother seemed docile but embarrassed by the actions of her brother. After that episode, Uncle Masood always seemed to respect the wishes of both our parents. Seemingly not respecting or even understanding most people, his wife, our aunt Mastoureh, was the one we all feared, including our parents. When she was over, she would often chastise Mother for her pictures of the queen and say, "She is not true to our Islamic heritage. She is *Shaytan (Satan)* or a troublemaker."

Mother would whisper, "Her dignity upholds all of us, and this, you know." We learned early from both our parents to stand our ground; thus, we can be effective without being loud.

Chapter 2
Northern New Jersey, Mid-1970s

"Ruth, come in here and see this," Ted Holmes announced to his wife on the early humid August, New Jersey evening of 1974. "Dick Nixon is on the news giving his farewell speech to his staff."

"Honey, I've got dinner ready…Richard, get your sisters—dinner's just about ready."

"Ruth…This is history. You and all the kids should come in and watch this."

With the Holmes family finding their way to the family room, allaying their appetites, the gray of the N.B.C. Nightly News blared out the dramatic speech.

Turning to her younger sister Maggie, Erin Holmes whispered, "Look at Mom."

Mrs. Holmes, now fully absorbed in the speech by the first American president ever to resign, had shifted her concentration from her homemade meatloaf and mashed potatoes. Tears roaming down her cheeks, Ruth Holmes, a dedicated Eugene McCarthy supporter in the previous presidential election, moaned, "Oh, he really was a good, kind man, listen to how he calls his mother a saint."

The precocious Maggie blurted out as only a confident middle school child could, "Mom, I thought you said he was a phony."

"Don't be disrespectful to your mother, and she's entitled to change her mind."

"But Dad…"

"No buts just listen and learn."

The Holmes family listened, as families did across America that summer evening. Perhaps just as historic as the president's resignation was the witnessing of the tender and sentimental side of the brooding president, who recently had embarrassingly announced, "I'm not a crook."

With the speech over, the family gathered around the table, digging into the carefully made meal. Ted Holmes, embracing a melancholy tone, commented, "Well, he was always my president. Not just because I'm a Republican, but he did accomplish a lot of important things—visiting China, accelerating the events that led us to have the first man on the moon…Hey, Richard—you're a Boy Scout, you do all that hiking upstate, Dick Nixon started an agency that protects the environment…"

"Daddy," Erin chimed in, "you call him Dick Nixon as if you know him personally."

"Your father was the coordinator of the Parade and dinner when President Nixon came to Eastwood in 1968."

"Wait a minute, Dad, you were? Wasn't Mom like a staunch Democrat?"

Looking at his wife affectionately, "Yes, the sexiest Democrat I ever saw."

"Ugggh! I think I'm going to get sick," revealed Maggie.

"Dad, stop," chimed Erin, "how did you guys get past that?"

"Not only that, your mother was the leader of *The New Jersey Youth for Stevenson Committee* before we got married."

"The what? Who was that?"

Richard intervened, "He was the guy who ran against Eisenhower in 1952 and 1956; we studied him last year in Civics class."

"Can I be excused…this adult talk is boring."

"Yes, Maggie, but remember you are helping with the dishes tonight."

Richard and Erin stayed put.

"Okay, I know you always say, Dad, that we live in a country where the best of friends can disagree on things, but you are like married and all, Mom, can you explain?"

"Explain what, dear?"

"Never mind, can I get up? I hate politics anyway."

With his sisters gone from the table and the conversation and safe from being accused of being a 'suck-up' by either or both of his sisters, Richard said, in a serious tone to his parents, "Mom, Dad, I think it's really cool that you both can be married and in love, and share different political opinions."

"You wouldn't just be trying to get out of taking out the garbage, would you, son?"

"No, seriously, it's impressive."

"I do have a request. Some of the boys from the cross-country team are meeting tomorrow night at 7:30 at the reservoir for a six-mile run. Can I skip dinner?"

"Richard, tomorrow your lifeguarding job is over at five. Can't you just run then?"

"Well, most of the others don't get off until after six, and we are really trying to beat the heat a little bit."

"Okay, but remember, one of these nights, your father and I would like to speak to you about colleges. After all, we only had that one visit to Rutgers and Villanova, and Coach Green thinks you can get a track scholarship to either one of those."

"Mom, Coach Green probably told you that, so you'll let me do late evening summer runs like tomorrow night. Besides, my mile time definitely has to be under 4:20 to get a scholarship to one of those programs. If I'm going to look at another school, it's really a smaller school that I'm interested in."

"Your father would not want me to say this, but he had such a great experience at Villanova. He would love it if you ended up there."

"Mom, okay, I'm looking at all those options we spoke about, but…"

"Okay, so you're agreeing to speak one night this week, then?"

"Yes."

Richard, a Northern Catholic High School senior, was the cross-country team's captain and vice-president of the History Club at school. Maintaining an average of ninety-one, he knew that if he put down the books he often gets lost in reading, he could really get his grades up to ninety-five or above and, as he felt, 'go where he really wanted'.

Two years younger than him, entering her sophomore year, Erin was already set on what she would study in college. Witnessing her uncle lose his life to lung cancer, she was determined to go into medicine, often announcing to her family, "If I don't find a cure for cancer, you know I'm going to come very close." When the fifteen-year-old Erin Holmes spoke like that, anybody listening within earshot who knew her knew she meant it.

Chapter 3
Mokashefeh

One day, Mahin surprised us all when she asked my mother, "Mother, why if you are a devoted Muslim, and you pray five times a day, why do you not have a picture in our house of our great Iranian martyr, Imam Hussein?"

Mother was indeed a devout Muslim and truly, the most spiritual person I had ever known in my life. As innately reserved as she was, she was sharp. One might say she was as 'dumb as a fox'. She knew this question did not grow organically from the recesses of my sister's mind.

"Thank you for asking me this very important question. Does your new friend Soraya have one in her home?"

Mother knew somehow that our aunt Mastoureh's next-door neighbor, a young girl who wore the full chador and carried the Quran wherever she went, was growing friendly to Mahin in recent months.

"Yes, and most of our neighbors do too, well, why don't we have this, we have the queen's picture?"

Mother's eyes, looking upwards, exclaimed, "We honor those deserving of the past in our hearts; we honor the future in the here and now?"

"Mother, what does that mean? It does not answer my question?"

"It does, most sufficiently, and you will ask no more of this."

During those months, Mahin seemed to bring home, framed in an angry tone, fervent questions of a religious nature. She asked my father how he could call himself 'A quiet Communist, how can you be a quiet anything?'

My father, forever maintaining the temperament of a well-contained sage, would reply, "It is good you are going to an American university; you will be able to absorb many different ideas, understand the world, and develop thoughts of your own, your journey will be one of *mokashefeh* or discovery."

We never knew just to what extent 'discovery' Mahin was actually going to undertake.

I often wondered if I was imagining things based on my concern about what was happening in my city. Simultaneously, there were rumors that the SAVAK, the Shah's police, was cracking down on dissidents, while mullahs, inspired by the exiled Khomeini, were creating militia-type groups who were accosting women without a headscarf, actually beating up and bruising several.

I thought of my father's comments and wondered why Mahin would be getting more hostile to my parents when she had the opportunity to go to a country where, from what we knew, things seemed more open and peaceful. They tolerated the growing questions given by Mahin on where my parents stood on matters of religion and state. However, one day, weeks before she was to leave for university in America, the professorial patience of father was severely tested.

"Girls, gather around. I have some wonderful news for you. Rather than go on our holiday trip to the Caspian shore, in two weeks' time, we will travel to *The Shiraz Art Festival.* We will be staying with cousin Talid and family...we will..."

"That is nothing but the propaganda of the imperialist monarchy. I want no part of that," announced Mahin.

Throwing a copy of *Ferdowsi* magazine and knocking over a cup of Mother's tea, Father grew blood red, as we had never witnessed. His voice rose from a yell to a scream, "You are becoming the dog of the adulterated mullahs and their false prophecies. This is our people's art...this is the home of our greatest poet, Hafiz."

Seeing the tumult she had caused with Mother weeping while Father screamed, Mahin quietly walked to our shared room. I went to comfort my mother, yet could not walk into the room I shared with my sisters. This sister was growing increasingly foreign to me before she even left our country.

Mahin did manage a show of contrition the next morning, speaking softly to both my parents on how she 'wished to visit the tomb of Hafez' while we were there. She never did apologize, nor did my father, for his outburst. We ended up going on the trip, and it was the greatest memory of my young life, particularly the time spent with our younger sister, Esteri.

Soon, Mahin would be off to university in America, in 'California', and I know it was an unspoken sigh of relief for my parents.

Chapter 4
A Father's Crisis

Richard Holmes had spent the last two years of high school accomplishing everything he had set out to. He had been 'ablaze as a distance runner'. *The Bergen County Blaze,* the *New Jersey Star-Ledger* dubbed him. When he was less than two seconds off former Paramus Catholic H.S. runner Tim Conheeney's Bergen County two-mile record, that performance run solidified a scholarship offer from Rutgers Gagliano. It did not hurt that his desired ninety-five average came his way after finally putting aside his favored history books for a greater focus on his calculus and senior statistics courses. Richard was all set to head to New Brunswick in the fall when coming out of the shower one night, and his mother shouted out to him, "Richard, there's a call on the phone for you."

"Is it Coach Gags?" Richard answered.

"No, it's the Villanova coach," Mrs. Holmes answered with affirmation.

Richard grabbed his towel and picked up the rotary phone, thinking it an obvious joke from one of his teammate friends, and said, "Hi!"

The low, monotone voice replied, "Hi, Richard, it is Jumbo Jim Elliot of Villanova."

For a serious moment, Richard was going to reply, "Wrong number, this is the King of England," but something told him it was perhaps the legendary coach who coached more Penn Relays champions and perhaps more Olympians than any coach alive. The voice went on, "I heard you ran a solid two-mile."

Richard knew this was the real deal, Coach Elliot.

After that call, there was no question that Richard would take up the offer and partial scholarship to run for the man who coached the great milers and Olympians Marty Liquori, Frank Murphy, and, currently, Eammon Coghlan.

No sound-thinking, young American schoolboy distance runner would pass up that opportunity. Richard would be pursuing his college education and joining the legacy of the Villanova greats come September.

The anticipated path to 'Wildcat greatness' eluded him in a near-fatal accident he was a victim of. While out on an early morning run with his good friend and teammate Jim Flynn on pastoral Montgomery Avenue, a car sideswiped him, thrown some fifty feet, and thanks to Flynn and his quick-thinking C.P.R., Richard was out of a concussion-induced coma. Richard saw the visions of victory 'hummm' by him in the back of an ambulance breezing through the hemlock-lined streets of the 'mainline' suburb. Running, needless to say, for Richard was over for at least a year. For the first time in his life, he was without a rigorous schedule, becoming a quiet participant in the myriad of 'keg parties' in and around the stately campus, counting the days to summertime when he could at least feel productive in his old lifeguard job. The summer he longed for to recover and rehabilitate, became one in which he would be tasked to rehabilitate and mend others.

Later that summer, Ted Holmes ventured to work on a humid August morning as he had for the past twenty-four years. Ted had survived three mergers as a loan officer for Bank Watterson, formerly an American-based bank, recently acquired by a London-based conglomerate. Ted's career and workdays were nearly mundane repetitions of routine. Every day he bought his coffee and buttered roll, *New York Times* and *Star-Ledger* at Walt's diner in town, boarded the 7:09 am train to Jersey City, took the Hudson tubes, and arrived at his midtown office no later than 8:40 am.

This Monday, there was time to speak about the weekend, the Yankees, and Richard's college choices with his closest associate at work, Mike Jenks. Jenks' daughter, Darlene, a junior in high school, was an outstanding swimmer. Jenks called her the 'best backstroker in Bergen County' and never stopped talking about how 'We are really hoping to get some scholarship calls thanks to this new Title IX'.

"It's a whole new world out there now…thank goodness for us."

Ted always thought, *Ironic as his memory did not fail him*—remembering three years prior how the discussion came up about women's rights one day at the office, Jenks distinctly blurted out, "Come on everybody, the women are getting all the perks. Next thing they will be awarding them athletic scholarships to colleges the way they give revenue-producing football players grants." Other than his primitive comments on that, he was Ted's 'goombah' at work since he was one of the last employees other than Ted to be with the company for more than twenty years. As Jenks put it to Ted one day at lunch, "There seems to be a bloated surplus of starched suits with pale faces and brutal British accents around the office these days." Although Jenks was a staunch Met fan, Ted a Yankee Fan; Jenks a Kennedy Democrat, Holmes a staunch old-school Republican, Jenks a self-proclaimed WASP, Ted a died-in-the-wool Roman Catholic—the men were close beyond work. As Ted told his wife one day, "I love the predictability of Mike."

Today, there would be an alarming unpredictability in Ted's life.

By this time in the morning, Ted had returned one call. Looking at his watch, he remembered it was 9:12 am, and his secretary, Helen Weinblatt, who had been with him at Watterson for twenty-one years, buzzed him, "Miss Harrison of the D.G.M'.s office is on the line."

"Mr. Holmes, Mr. Winchester would like to see you upstairs in his office at 10:00 am."

"I'll be there."

Ted wondered what it could be about. He had not even met the twenty-seven-year-old deputy general manager at the company Christmas party or the spring social, they held for 'achieving quarterly record earnings'. Ruminating to himself, Holmes was certain it was not about performance, as he had just been rewarded with a performance raise in June.

After the interminably long forty minutes, Ted still found himself sitting in the waiting room of the D.G.M'.s 45th-floor office.

"You may go in," the well-coiffed secretary announced.

Laying eyes on Albert Winchester for the second time this year since the young British transplant had arrived, Ted immediately reflected on Mike Jenks' 'starched suit' comment. Apart from the young man who sat in front of him, or the office he sat in, there was nothing remotely inspiring other than the starched brown suit.

Without even a hello, Winchester smoothly stated, "The severance package is indeed a good one. Studies show it is the most generous in the banking industry, indeed, we would want to have it that way, especially for long-term employees like yourself."

Ted returned, "Severance package, is this a topic we will be presenting to our middle managers at our weekly meeting downstairs?"

Ted was not trying to be coy; for several moments, he would not have a 'foggy idea' what Winchester was talking about. After all, Winchester used that term.

"I'm not sure I have a foggy idea of what you are talking about, Mr. Holmes?"

When the confusion in the room was put to rest for both of the inhabitants, the ache in Ted's gut allowed him to pursue the practice of what he always told his children. "When you are in the right, be calm, but don't back down from speaking your mind respectfully, but loudly."

"Mr. Winchester, sir, what are you telling me here? The nebulousness is undeserving to me or any dedicated employee?"

"Mr. Holmes, let's be adults here, as a 'dedicated employee', you more than understand company decisions are made on the highest level, and I've welcomed you to my office to give you that two weeks' notice."

"What, are you telling me I'm fired? Is that it? Despite my numbers being the second highest company-wide performer, as told to me, at the offering of my pay raise bonus in June?"

"Mr. Holmes, we are all expendable, and I hastened to say our time is done here."

Ted remembered himself staying calm, or at least telling himself that.

"What is this payback for our victory in the American Revolution? This curtness is how you treat employees?"

"Mr. Holmes, we are finished here. Shall I request security?"

Ted got up, straightened his shoulders, and looked at Winchester and the room, straining shortly, looking in disbelief at the blandness of the man, the room, and the man's message. As he walked through Winchester's door, he thought to himself, "Jenks was right; it's a whole new world out there."

Chapter 5
Parent's Blessings

Mother's influence over our father was uncanny. She was quietly charismatic in both our house and our neighborhood, and her ability to draw others to do what she felt was right was nothing short of incredible. This was most evident when my parents announced in the summer of 1977 that they would both be going to *Hajij*. Esteri and I could not believe what we were hearing.

"Father, too?" We both inquired.

"Yes, your father has realized it is best in the interest of praying for not only our family and our country but also for your sister in her travels and education."

It was by that comment that I realized that they had both grown in concern about my sister's 'travels'. Rather than come home from her American university that summer, she wrote to her mother and father that she was 'selected by the government to do some studies and surveys in Lebanon'. Her letter and her subsequent responses were extremely vague, causing the concern that our parents felt they were keeping from us. Whether this encouraged the father to seek religion or not, it most certainly was one of the reasons.

Our grandparents, Mashid and Rasool Biniaz, would be coming from Isfahan, a city south of Tehran, to stay with us. This was a special time as our grandmother was an incredible cook, and our uncle was perhaps the funniest man I had ever met in my life. Almost nightly after dinner, Grandfather Rasool would close the blinds, bang the walls, look under the sofa and furniture as if checking for listening devices placed by phantom members of the SAVAK, and then proceed to go into a hilarious routine impersonating the Shah. Esteri and I would be in stitches as Grandmother cleaned up the table and dinner plates. While we loved our father dearly, we had never witnessed a man employ humor. We also knew full well that this was a secret event for our eyes only, and word of it could never even be told to our parents. While Mother loved Queen Farah, she would often lament, "If only he could be as pure as she," and then in a loud voice, with arms up to God, shout out, *Chi shad?*

"What happened?" My father tolerated the Shah and always saw the good in others, even dictators, and lauded his accomplishments for the benefit of 'the people'. Perhaps father's pragmatism was paramount. In a growing society where neighbors seemed increasingly paranoid of what was said in public discourse, my father often said, *Divar moosh dare va moosh ham goosh dare.* This was an old Persian saying meaning, 'The walls have mice, and the mice have ears'.

Grandmother Madhid was a great quilter, and Grandfather Rasool was a lover of books and loved to tell us stories from the most recent books he had read. While Esteri would listen for hours to Grandfather's stories and seemed to be totally captivated by them, I drew closer to Grandmother. Grandmother had a terrible cough, and there were nights when she asked me to place hot clothes on her chest. Her feet also swelled almost daily, and I would gently massage them. She would call me *Al-Mu'alijah,* healer. I had often contemplated medical studies, as it gave me great satisfaction that I could bring soothing relief to a person I cherished. Spending time with them was so very special that my sister and I had to feign excitement when Mother and Father came home. It also signaled the time that our year of school studies would begin.

That summer, significant changes were happening in our Tehran. The traffic was getting worse, 'unbearable', as my mother would put it, and there seemed to be students protesting on a daily basis at the University of Tehran. Esteri and I would often walk by them with great interest. Most of those protests were against the Shah. However, one day, there was a group of men who looked noticeably older than the other students, shouting sentiments and showing placards against the exiled cleric in Najaf, Mullah Khomeini. It was actually the first time we had heard his name aloud since Father forbade, several years earlier, our uncle from coming over and playing his tapes. Father, I recalled, seethed at the man's name. One of my friends, Fahimeh, told me that her father said those men were actually agents of the SAVAK masquerading as students. It was the first time I remembered being frightened by things happening around us. It was perhaps then and there that I decided if

I had the opportunity, I would seek a university education out of the country just like my sister.

I knew full well this would be particularly difficult for my parents to understand due to Mahin's increasing alienation from us. The only correspondence in the previous two months was a letter from her telling us how she received an A+ in her 'Political Culture' seminar class for her thesis on the 'Parable of Persepolis'. She went on an impersonal rant describing how she researched the party the Shah put on to celebrate the 2500th year of a reigning monarchy in 1971. The event was an over-the-top affair where tents were made and flown in from France, thousands of trees and plants, and legions of food were also flown in. A foreign retinue of heads of state was flown in from all over the globe, including the Emperors of Ethiopia, members of the British Royal family, the American vice-president, the kings and queens of Denmark, Norway, Jordan, Greece, Prince Rainier and Princess Grace of Monaco, and others. The guests were picked up at the airport by over two hundred and fifty Mercedes-Benz limousines and dined for hours as musicians and dancers performed. She wrote this was '…a lesson for all Iranians of the indulgent decadence of the exploitive Shah and his family'. Quoting the exiled Ayatollah Khomeini, she wrote, "This excessive expenditure satisfying the Shah's greed was another example of 'his rape of Iran'." She went on to say her professor proclaimed it to be 'the talk of U.C.L.A'. Reading what seemed more like a newspaper review than a letter to her family, Father stared into space, saying to no one in particular, "What have the Americans done to our daughter?"

Father's oldest brother, Ebrahim, was a professor at the 'Abadan Institute of Technology' and had visited that summer, as he always had. He was calm and wise, and I know his mother and father respected him well. I told him of my plans that after my first year at Ferdowsi University in Mashhad for pre-medical studies, I would perhaps transfer to a university abroad. He suggested I tell my parents right away of the plan, giving them time to digest it and 'softening the sentimental blow'. He then told me, "Aunt Nazarin and I would like you girls to come to Abadan next summer to visit with us." Uncle Ebrahim and Aunt Nazarin were our favorite aunts and uncles, and we always felt bad that they had no children of their own.

Heeding Uncle Ebrahim's advice encouraging me to pursue education abroad, I waited one night after dinner, when Mother and Father had the music of the Golha playing softly, to tell them of my desire to go to university abroad. I remember my mother getting up, moaning out, *Pigeon with pigeon, falcon with falcon.* In other words, 'Birds of a feather flock together'. My mother could not bring herself to speak to me. Father stayed calm and collected as usual and explained how hard it has been on them with Mahin leaving and 'not even coming back this summer…her letter writing has become less and less'. When she came back to my room, I assured him and mother, sufficiently gathered, sitting on the bed, that 'Mahin was the oldest and independent one'.

"Mother, Father, I need you, I need us, I need Iran…perhaps what I seek is different from Mahin, I need a self-reaffirmation of that…if I go, it is for an answer that for my family, me, and yes, our beloved Iran that we can do better." I boldly announced, "My career is definitive. It is not philosophical…I want to get the best medical studies I can to help our people, help our culture."

To that, the three of us hugged. I knew I had their blessings to pursue my education where I wanted—a year of medical studies in Mashhad—followed by education abroad, of course, if I qualified, and what I desired most—an undistracted education.

Chapter 6
Health Scare

Richard was calmly ecstatic to be back home from school for the summer. Although he initially had to endure well-meaning neighbors greeting him with spiced welcomes such as 'Hey Blaze, great to see you, how many records did you break down there at Villanova', having a chance to see and hang out with old teammates and friends was what Richard craved for. All his friends were home for the summer except for Lou Cifarelli, who was always ambitious. Lou was doing a summer business internship in Boston he received through his college, Williams. In addition to being the collegiate freshman with the biggest eyes on his future, Lou was the most generous among his friends. With his first summer paycheck, he had already bought six tickets for Richard, himself, and their friends to a 23 July Harry Chapin concert at the South Shore Music Circus right outside of Boston. When Richard asked, "How are we all going to come up and stay for the weekend?"

"No worries, I met a great UMass girl whose family has a place on Mason's Island off the eastern coast of Connecticut, and she told me 'they would welcome us any weekend in the summer'."

Tommy Gaffak, the North Catholic H.S. team member who drifted the furthest from Jersey to go to school, Willamette University in Oregon, was already planning to reciprocate as the guys got together that first night mid-June at Tommy's house in Upper Saddle River. Gaffak had a backyard built-in pool and an advanced cannonball dive to prove he spent more than a few minutes in it.

Gaffak announced, "Remember Billy Stephens, the football player two years older than us?"

"Of course, the guy who came out his senior year and threw the shot over 55' at the All Groups Meet?"

"Yeah, well, he is playing ball for Temple now, and this summer, he's working as a bouncer at The Stone Pony in Asbury Park. The hottest group down there, Southside Johnny and the Asbury Jukes is playing some nights this summer with this guy from Freehold, and he is outstanding."

Donnie Tricario chimed in, "That's the guy Bruce everybody down there says is going to be even bigger than the Jukes."

Holding a Miller bottle, Tommie shouted, "Guys, will all present join me in toasting to the most awesome guy summer in history!"

The loud and deafening cheers were followed by a team cannonball, creating splashes seemingly squirting toward the vastness of the optimistic moonlit sky.

It was a great night for Richard to forget about his injury and disappointing freshman year and enjoy a promising summer.

Coming home that evening, Richard was immediately overtaken by the ashen look on his mother's face that he would never forget. Her eyeliner was smeared and dried on her upper left cheek, clearly from tears. He had never seen his mother in such a state.

"Richard, I need to tell you something…I wanted to tell you and your sisters, but I could not bring myself to tell them…so I allowed them to go with Jeannie Rafferty to the mall and out for the night." Jeannie Rafferty was the family baby-sitter when the kids were young; now, in her last year at Boston College, she was actually someone who the family hadn't been close to in recent years.

"Mom, what happened…I know it's not good."

"Mrs. Weinblatt, your father's longtime secretary, called this afternoon to tell me they laid off your father from work."

"Whaaat? I thought Dad was like the superstar there…"

"He was, I mean, he is, but he had premonitions of bad things happening to his division when the British took over the company."

"Damn them! How is Dad…what has he said?"

"I haven't heard from him…I can feel his pain…" Ruth Holmes muttered as she was now in total tears.

"Mom, have you tried calling Mr. Jenks?"

"I will as soon as I get myself together."

In his first act of serving as a pillar of strength and stability in the family, Richard announced, "Mom, would it be easier for you if I call him?"

"Oh, yes, please, Richard."

It was now well past commuting time, so Richard knew enough to call him at home. With his daughter, Darlene, answering, Richard praised her swimming exploits, ignoring the freshman-year crush he had on her and how shy he was at neighborhood barbecues she was at. She rambled on about her scholarship offers, and Richard cut her off impolitely, asking to speak to her father. There was what seemed to be an interminable time before Mr. Jenks got on the line, speaking in an uncharacteristically solemn tone.

"Richard…how's the old Blaze himself?"

"Fine, Mr. Jenks, but I'm calling—"

"Richard, I know what you're calling about. We are all shocked about the way, well, not even the way, the actual act of your father being terminated…without any prior hint."

"Mr. Jenks…can you tell me why?"

"Richard, excuse my French; I know you are a good Villanova boy, but nobody has a clue why they would fire the fucking best employee in the division, if not the company…I don't know what to tell you, and many of us are wondering what it bodes for us."

"Mr. Jenks, can you tell me where my dad is?"

"Richard, I'm sorry…I left him hours ago. We were just having a few, well, we were just…"

"Drinks?"

"Yes, Richard, considering the circumstances…we, well, your dad was drowning out the pain, I guess you would say."

"Is he alright?"

"Well, when I left him, he was…we were at McSorley's…Richard, I should get off the wire now…listen, anything I can do to help you and your family…he's always been so proud of you…he worried about you though this year with your injury and all."

Richard got off the phone, punched the stucco wall by the mud room, and screamed from deep in his gut, "Who are these fuckers?"

"Richard, please, I need you to be calm, please…"

"Mom, I'm sorry, I'm going to drive in the city…"

"Richard, you are not going to do that at all. If your dad's not home by eleven, I'm calling the police."

Before Ruth Holmes barely finished her sentence, the phone rang. They both stared a long moment before Ruth grabbed the phone.

"Mrs. Holmes, this is Dr. Savood Sinders. I am calling from the Emergency Room at Mt. Sinai Hospital."

"Yes—"

"Your husband Theodore is in stable condition, but he was experiencing some chest discomfort and a little dizziness at the restaurant he was in, and thank goodness, the owner had him ambulanced over here."

"We will be on our way."

Richard immediately called his uncle Ryan, who was a retired F.B.I agent living in Ridgewood—

"Rich—don't worry—I'll bring my badge—we'll speed—we'll get in right to see him." The three drove into the city. Erin and Maggie, walking into the conflagration of tension in the house, insisted on coming, but Ruth had already made one call, and several neighbors came to be with and watch them both.

When they arrived at the hospital, they were relieved to see Ted up and talking to the nurses and Dr. Sinders. What Richard remembers most is that evening in the hospital was the last time he saw his father. He remembered growing up happy, energetic, and vibrant with life.

Chapter 7
Mother's Emotions

In the spring, I received notice that Georgetown University had accepted me into their nursing exchange program through Ferdowsi University. Mother, the day before, had handed me the envelope with a stained postage mark. It was quite obvious it was a tear-induced stain. Father seemed proud. Waiting for Father to be out the next day and Esteri with her friends in the outer room, I took it upon myself to speak to Mother.

"Mother, you must believe what I have told you. I seek to make the most out of myself and come back to our country and serve our people."

"Like your sister did?"

"Mother, she went to California…they say that is not even America… people have much, much too much, and they live in decadence."

"Now you speak like Mahin."

"Mother, all I'm saying is that my purpose has always been definitive…my love for my family is always forever."

"Well, as the Imam told us at Hajij—'the true believer should not make mistakes and apologize', I will say no more."

"Mother, you and Father gave me your blessing last summer, and I will take that with me. You must do the same and take my promise with you, and please let us make the most of our peace and our place here while we are at home."

As I finished saying that, there was yet another protest right outside our window. Father rushed into the house out of breath, saying there were thousands shouting, "Marg bar Shah—down with the Shah." Mother perplexedly said, "I don't understand this. The queen just yesterday walked the streets, with a woman showering her with hugs and kisses and thanking her for her unwavering charity."

"Mother, why don't you understand? Farah represents everything good about our country: family, charity, love, and devotion, whereas Reza Pahlavi represents nearly the opposite—the complexities and the reliance on outside influencers in our country."

"As I said earlier, now you speak like Mahin."

At that point, Father blurted out, "Speaking of Mahin, I have wonderful news."

"What is it, Father?" Esteri and I shouted at the same time.

"Your sister Mahin will be home next week. Uncle Ebrahim and Aunt Nazarin have invited Esteri and your favorite cousin, Somaya, Talid's daughter, to stay with them in Abadan in mid-August."

"Husband, we have not spoken about this invitation."

Father immediately turned to Mother, saying, "Now, my woman of the angels, one of us will be able to leave the stifling Tehran heat and pollution, and she will be back before Shideh leaves the country."

Father went on, "Abadan will be a wonderful place for the girls to visit in the summer. It is absent of political strife. What do we only see on the streets of Tehran now? We see traffic-the traffic of unrest and violence. The darkness of the chador is not meant to be the one and only color one can see in the shadows of the Alborz." I remember all too well those prescient words of Father.

Mahin came and went. On her first night home, while her mother was cooking, she critically perused the kitchen, telling her mother, "I see you are still content with your pictures of Shahbanouh in your house."

Eternally avoiding any discord, Mother sheepishly answered, "Yes, she still shines, doesn't she…could you bring the lamb over? Thanks."

About to verbally retaliate, Mahin was stopped dead in her bitter tracks as her mother calmly continued, "It's wonderful that through the Pahlavi Foundation, you have been afforded a scholarship to a foreign university."

That seemed to render my bold sister tongue-tied for at least one more day.

The next night at dinner after Friday prayers, Mother asked, "Mahin, whatever became of the next-door neighbor of Mastoureh?"

Mahin became solemn for several seconds. "Do you mean my friend, Soraya?"

"Yes, we have not seen her for quite some time."

"And you will not see her for quite some time more," Mahin answered dramatically.

"She was killed in Lebanon."

"Lebanon?" We all responded.

"Yes, fighting for the cause of Allah."

Father implored, "I'm not sure we understand what you are saying, Mahin."

Mahin's response to Father was unforgettable and unforgivable.

"Of course, you do not understand, Father. While you drive your Paykin and teach your mathematics, your Shah drives the American-bought limousine out of his gilded, lined, corrupt palace past the places of poverty in our streets, not seeing the faces of Iranian despair."

Mahin went on in her diatribe, "There is going to be a *defa-e-mogaddar*, a sacred defense of our freedoms, and we will rise up. Where will you be, Father?"

Unexpectedly and out of character, Mother got up, "I know where we will be with our family, our loved ones, with the Quran, not with what spews from your hateful foreign-produced mind. I am disgraced to say this to the eldest of my beautiful daughters, but you are no longer welcome at this table until you find peace within yourself."

The thing I remember most about that night is that we had never witnessed extreme emotions from Mother. That night, we had seen Mother emote a visceral feeling for the first time, yet she did not shed a tear. I always imagined after that night that Mother had previously shed a million tears quietly in her room, in her prayers over the past three years over the anguish of the alienation from her eldest daughter, Mahin.

Chapter 8
Heart and Soul

There would be no Harry Chapin concert with his good, loyal friends or any planned 'awesome guy trips' other than a quick day beach trip to Asbury Park with Tommy Gaffak. Nor would there be any good times down at 'The Stone Pony', as Richard and his family became increasingly overwrought with the deteriorating condition of Ted Holmes.

Ruth booked a week for the family at the Essex and Sussex, a grand, old-world hotel in Spring Lake, New Jersey, in late July. With the hotel sitting across the street from the Atlantic Ocean, Ruth hoped just merely sitting out on the hotel's exquisite Victorian wrap-around porch would be cathartic for the ailing husband and father. She envisioned the fresh, salty sea air would bring color and life back into Ted's pallid mien. The hotel was rumored to be 'hanging on' as one of the sole stately properties left on the Jersey Shore. She knew Ted's parents used to bring him and his brother and sister down there every summer when they were young. Ruth was determined to bring the vibrant life and spirit she had known in Ted since her college days at Marymount back to normal. She had witnessed that spark wilt away before her very eyes in just a few weeks.

Richard and Ted were able to go fishing on a chartered boat out of the Shark River. Midway through the fishing trip, Ted asked Richard to get him a beer. Knowing this probably wouldn't be the best thing for his dad at this time, Richard hesitated, and most likely sensing this, Ted called him back.

"Richard—don't bother. I totally feel even with one beer, and I'll be sleeping with the fishes." The indirect reference to 'The Godfather', his father's favorite movie, gave Richard a glimmer of hope that perhaps his dad's wit and memory were back for good. But things slowly morphed into a morbid conversation after that.

"You know, Richard, I am so damn proud of you, I can't even describe it. You know you have your mother's fight within you. I'll never forget when you came charging down that last stretch in that state cross-country meet to beat that Bound Brook kid at literally the finish line—we could see your face of grit—I'm so proud, so, so proud of you."

"Thanks, Dad, and I of you."

"Well, you can't be too proud of your sickly, unemployed father now."

"Dad, this is just a temporary thing; Mr. Jenks said you were the best fucking employee in the company."

"Ha—sounds exactly what old Mike would say."

"Dad, what did happen? Why would they let you go?"

"Richard, companies just want to shift things up to make it look like new management is doing something. Two pieces of advice I can give you—don't piss off the British, work hard and work honestly, but give your heart and soul to your family and your faith, never to your company or even your country…they'll rip it from you and drive on and say, 'Happy motoring'."

"What, Dad?"

"Sounds harsh and rather unpatriotic for an old Republican like yourself."

Staring with a look in his eyes that Richard would never forget, Ted went on, "Again…give your heart and soul to your family, everything will take care of itself from there…Work hard, be true, but no company, no country is noble enough to own your heart and soul."

Ted put his arm around Richard. "So, will you please promise me you'll take care of Erin, Maggie, and your mom?"

Holding back tears at the finality of the sage advice and parental request, Richard could only mutter, "Yeah, Dad, of course, yeah, always."

The Holmes family was able to enjoy a fantastic week—water-skiing, body surfing, going down to Asbury Park for the rides, enjoying the 'world's best custard' sold every night on the boardwalk, and loving life together. The air of carnival, along with the salty aroma of the mist from the crashing Atlantic, was cathartic to anybody walking on the Asbury Park boardwalk. The giant enigmatic clown face engraved on the wall of the Convention Hall contradicted the solemn feelings. Richard felt viscerally after his fishing trip conversation with his dad.

Those feelings would meet with external reality as two weeks after the unforgettable family trip, Ted Holmes succumbed to a massive heart attack in the living room of their Eastwood home.

It was a momentary shock for Richard. Had it not been for the time and conversation on the fishing trip with his father, he would have been without preparation for his great loss. It was then and there that he realized his father had a sense of his short time left on earth, and his words to Richard filled the lacunae Richard had often felt during his youth with his hard-working success consumed father.

The lines outside the funeral home for both nights of the wake wrapped around the block. Midway through the crowd the second night, a tall, distinguished, but hunched man approached Richard and his mother. Richard assumed the man was hunched forward because his back was bothering him from waiting in the long line outside on the hot, humid August night. The man leaned over and grunted something indistinguishable but seemingly very sincere.

Ruth, in a nearly excited tone, addressed the man.

"Bill, thank you so much for making the trip…it means so much to us…Richard, get Mr. Casey a chair."

Richard complied, and the snow cover of dandruff on the man's shoulder triggered a memory within him of when he saw him last. It was when Richard was ten, and his parents forced him and his sisters to attend an Opera at Fordham University, and that man and his wife sat in front of him.

The man, this Mr. Casey, got up after a few minutes, grunted something Richard discerned as 'You are your dad's man', kneeled, said a prayer at the coffin, and kissed Ruth, who was now receiving the mayor of Eastwood's respects, goodbye.

When the last of the people came through somewhere after 11:00 pm, Uncle Ryan came up to Richard, asking, "What the hell did Casey say to you?"

"Well, I'm not totally sure, but something to the extent of 'you are your father's man'…who is he anyway? He seemed out of it, but at the same time, he seemed really important or something?"

"That's Bill Casey—he sure as hell is. He was a great friend of your dad's from Fordham. He's one of the original OSS intelligence guys, now a big-time lawyer, former Secretary of the Securities Exchange Commission, a friend of

Nixon's, and advisor to President Ford. Your dad always said he was the smartest guy in the room, in any room, at all times."

"Wow—how come if Dad thought that of him, and he liked Dad so much—he never came to the house?"

"He did when you were younger—they really hit it off—but he travels too much apparently now…your dad worked with him and saw a lot of him at Fordham alumni events."

"Oh yeah, those far too many events which Dad felt compelled to go to and give his heart and soul to. I don't think the university ever appreciated the volunteer work he did for them. I used to get mad because he missed so many of my ball games for that stuff. His heart and soul—you know Dad didn't live up to the advice he gave to me…"

"What was that advice, Richard?"

"Oh, never mind, Uncle Ryan, I'm starting to be a crybaby."

"You're allowed, Richard, you're allowed. Your dad knew I always wished I had a son like you or a daughter like your sisters…he knew that."

"Uncle Ryan, are my mom and my sisters going to be all right?"

"Richard, your dad even knew the answer to that—yes—because he is alive in you!"

Chapter 9
Abadan Horror

Father was quite excited about his brother and sister-in-law's invitation to Esteri to spend some time with them in Abadan. I always felt that Esteri was the apple of my father's eye. She was brighter than Mahin and I, and yet she was not as 'disruptive'. Mother always said that "Mahin and I were handfuls growing up," but at least "the fire inside of you, Shideh, has subsided with your advancing years." Esteri, however, was almost too good. I can never remember when she caused worry or concern for my parents over her studies or behavior. Never.

The plan was for Esteri to take a train from Tehran to Shiraz, where our aunt and uncle would pick her and cousin Somaya up. We always understood Uncle Ebrahim to be 'of means', and he insisted on paying for all transportation of Esteri and Somaya, and 'wherever the girls wanted to be taken with Nazarin, they are not to consider spending any of their own money'. It was understood that our aunt, as custom has it, would be taking them to the bazaar, the shore to swim, and even the movie. Uncle Ebrahim would take them to visit the port, the holy shrines, and the university he taught at.

Esteri was the most intellectually curious of us. She would constantly be the one to ask questions about our culture and our government, always listening to others. I think the trip to Uncle Ebrahim's and Aunt Nazarin's was an extension of her curiosity; this we actually know because we have her diary, and the last entry she put in it the morning she left was 'I shall be the first one in my family to travel this far in our own vast country this young…I'm not sure Mother or Father have even been on a train'. While I loved my aunt and uncle, I'm not sure I would have accepted their invitation to visit them in the even hotter Abadan. Esteri, in that sense, was more adventurous.

The week before Esteri left, Mother was not sleeping but rather involved in *Qiyam-ul-layl,* or voluntary prayers, where she would stand through the night praying in addition to her daily prayers. Father, on the other hand, seemed giddy that his youngest daughter would be spending time with, as he put it, 'the smart brother' and learning more about the place and history of the country he loved so much. By that summer, he felt so strongly that the mood in Tehran was so angry and violent that it would serve anybody well to leave Tehran for some time, especially if it were somewhere in the country known to be more apolitical.

We also heard Father say how sensitive he was to his brother and his wife, who wanted children and could not conceive, and how much they really loved Mahin, myself, and Esteri as 'their own'. He knew that his brother would make the girl's trip as much an educational and cultural experience as possible.

"Aunt Nazarin will be taking you to the theater, and both of them will be taking you to some shrines…you are fortunate as the theaters in Tehran at this time," he said so memorably ironic, "are much too unsafe." Father then told us how he 'misses cinema much' and that the last film he saw in a theater was Downpour. He regaled us with stories of great Iranian filmmakers such as Bahram Beyzai. The excitement in Father's voice made us wish we were all traveling with Esteri just to visit the cinema.

The day Esteri left, we were so busy giving hugs that I could only think of the impossibility of my leaving in a couple of weeks for a place much farther away and still so much unknown to my family and me. I'll never forget Esteri looking straight up at me with her beautiful caramel eyes, saying so proudly, "Shideh, I can give you strength for your journey with my stories." She was years ahead of her age.

Two days into the trip, Esteri had called us, sounding like she and Somaya were having the time of their lives. She didn't speak long, just exclaiming how 'hot it was and how they looked forward to going to the cinema tomorrow night'. When my parents got off the phone, Esteri, giggling, told me, "Don't tell Mother or Father, but the movie Gavaznha, The Deer, stars the most famous and most handsome of all Iranian actors, Behrouz Vozzoughi." She was still a teenage girl. I was the last one to say *shab belcheir*, good night to Esteri.

Mother had not even finished her Shurooq sunrise prayers the next morning, and the phone rang. It rang again. I remember thinking I was dreaming. Initially, she felt no obligation to answer it. But then, she told me later, and she knew this early phone call could not mean anything good. Picking it up, she noticed before she heard a voice her left hand was shaking. Uncle Ebrahim was on the other line, crying. He could not muster two sentences together.

Mother's wail woke me up, and Father was trembling…they were screaming together, "Esteri, Somaya, why?"

Arsonists had purposely locked the doors of the Cinema Rex and pre-meditatively poured engine fuel in four corners, setting the theater ablaze. Somehow, one hundred movie watchers made it out on the roof and managed to escape. Over four hundred did not, either killed by smoke asphyxiation, being burned alive, or being trampled to death in the mad rush to live, to escape. My beautiful sister Esteri, cousin Somaya, and Aunt Nazarin perished. It would take us years to find out the full truth of this horrible, barbaric tragedy. But for me, it was the day my family, as I knew it, died.

Chapter 10
A Son's New Responsibility

"Richard, can you help me leaf through these papers—I need to check Dad's insurance policy. Do you think you can spend a couple of hours with me today going through some paperwork?"

"Mom, don't worry about a thing; I've already made my mind up. I'm going to be around for you this year, and I'm taking the year off to help you and the girls get through this."

"Richard, that's so loving of you, but you can't do that—you need to get your education, and your dad would have wanted to see you running, what you love to do once you get healthy."

"Mom, it's already been decided. I'm going to be working some hours for Uncle Ryan's security firm."

"I've spoken to him, Mom, it's a done deal. I couldn't live with myself knowing that you, Maggie, and Erin in her senior year of high school would be alone…unless, of course, you want me to go back to the business classes that I wonder why I'm taking, the keg parties, and the time with all the pretty girls…"

"Ok, Richard, have it your way…the girls could use your support, but how about a semester only?"

"Let's see how it works out, Mom…I just want to do the right thing for you."

Ruth, breaking up, "You always have, Richard, you always have."

Ryan Holmes finished an illustrious career with the New York Field Office of the F.B.I. He felt his thirty years with the agency flew by 'like a spring cardinal in the Meadowlands'. His first year in retirement was spent driving his wife to the Garden State Mall, attending a few plays in New York City, visiting relatives, mostly his in-laws down South, and playing too much-

uninspired golf. One day, after lunch with his retired New Jersey State Trooper friend, George Shea, Ryan announced, "Retirement isn't what it was cracked out to be."

"Holmsie, you're singing to the choir. You know, we tried the Florida thing for two years, and Joannie hated it…she couldn't wait to move back to Jersey…I never thought I lived to see and hear that."

Holmes was also harboring some guilt that maybe instead of doing the perfunctory 'retirement obligations', he should have found more time to spend with his most local of relatives, his now deceased brother Ted, and his family. Ryan told Shea that he had an idea to start a security agency and would love to have Shea join him in any capacity he desired. Shea reminded Holmes that he might find convincing his wife, May, a little bit challenging. Shea proposed that if he meets any resistance from her, 'just relay our aborted Florida retirement calamity…she can always speak to Joannie about that'.

There would be no resistance from May. She merely requested they keep their membership in the country club so she could keep playing tennis, and while 'he didn't have to try and impress and keep playing bad golf, at least let's keep attending the dances and socials'.

This was music to Ryan's ears. While he loved the F.B.I. and the time he spent there, he longed to use his F.B.I. expertise and be his own boss without answering bureaucratic red tape. It was a bonus to have a guy with a wealth of experience and contacts like George Shea interested in joining him in the venture. It was an added blessing when his own favorite and trusted nephew, Richard, asked him if he could work for him. Holmes suggested that he finish his college education with a transfer to Fairleigh Dickinson University, a college less than a half hour away from Richard's home, and work nights. Richard thanked him for the idea but told him he wanted to dedicate his free time to helping his mom and driving his sisters to their games and such.

"Richard, that is why your dad was so proud of you—your incredible sense of responsibility."

Two weeks past the funeral, the grief stage kicked in and kicked in fierce for Ruth. There would be no conversation that was not laden with, "I cannot believe your father is gone. I just cannot believe he is gone." As much as he knew he needed to comfort his despondent mother, Richard found he was asking his uncle for full-time hours with his agency.

Ryan set up an office in Carteret, New Jersey, a stone's throw from Manhattan. He originally performed private investigations, surveillance servicing, guarding buildings, and perhaps aiding any local police municipalities in criminal investigations. He would hire recently retired law enforcement men like himself. There would be jobs requiring both armed and unarmed security—so Richard needed to get his handgun license.

"Rich, I know you don't mind those nights doing mall guarding. I know you get a chance to read, but there is going to be a lot more action coming than being a mall dog if you're interested?"

"Uncle Ryan, of course, I am…sign me up."

"Well, Rich, you are the youngest guy in the agency, and that is fine, but you got to get your handgun license…you most likely will never have to use it, but it gives the agency more credibility if we say all our guys are licensed."

"Absolutely, I kind of figured that, but could we keep that secret from my mom…she's sorting out enough lately."

"What goes on in the agency, Richard, stays in the agency."

That wouldn't be the last time Richard would hear that line over the next few decades.

Chapter 11
Unspeakable Grief

The neighbors came in, setting up black candles around our house. I just remember in the face of this horrible, senseless tragedy—the death of my youngest sister, cousin, aunt, and hundreds of others, everybody seemed absorbed in surreal cultural realities. Fasting and praying would be the order of the next few days. Father was concerned about paying the death tax and making sure the mullahs were paid. "Mullah Ghaznavi must be paid," Father announced before the cleric came to lead the *nemaz e meyet,* or the prayer of death. Mother was concerned with getting the *kafan*, the traditional white cotton cloth to wrap the dead bodies in. But there were no dead bodies to be wrapped in. We were told that the theater was 'a giant box of ashes', human ashes. Father would be leaving after the second night to Abadan. We had seen the pictures, we had spoken to friends, and we had heard the voice of Uncle Ebrahim, his voice aging over two days, like that of a ninety-year-old man on his deathbed. There was no need for Father to go. But he insisted that he 'wanted to pray where his daughter breathed her last breath'.

Mother carried herself in a strange ritualistic manner. When we broke our fast, she constantly reminded us of the right food to be out for the guest mourners and us. She was constantly going in and folding Esteri's clothes. These unnecessary absurdities were only a hint of the grief that she would display not just for the next forty days but forever. I think that at the time, worrying about my mother allayed my grief, which I would not face entirely until years later. There were flocks of people coming to our door expressing condolences and prayer. Since Tehran had already been shrouded in black due to the anticipation of the overthrow of the Shah and his 'Western ways', there was no telling if all the black worn was for the death of Esteri or for societal propriety. Since there was no accurate accounting of not just who died but how many, we did not know if anybody else from Tehran was in the Abadan Theater that night. It was a long way away, and neighbors and friends lamented why it had to happen on what was supposed to be an 'enriching visit with relatives'. Aunt Mastoureh brought that point up. She also was heard saying, "My only relief is knowing that their deaths were immediate and painless." There was nothing immediate and painless enough in death by asphyxiation. Her lack of logic transcended her hatred for the Shah.

When Mahin arrived, it made the dizzying spell-like trance I was in temporarily disappear. Ironically, we conversed as we had not in years. We recounted the stories of when Esteri first walked, of when she was found in mother's cooking area with a pie over her face, and when at six, she dazzled all of us with her questions of the sky and 'Allah swerving around all the time up there'. We knew then she was appropriately named. Father announced, "She is truly a child of the stars." Mahin spoke about how she knew from that day forward that Esteri was the favored child. She was, of course, the one who loved more than anyone to go with her father to museum visits. Looking back, I joked to Mahin that I almost felt we were delinquents next to our sister, a child of wonder and innocence. Speaking to Mahin helped put my head back out of the orbit of despair I was floating in. We were all not only robbed of a life we loved but of the energy that we almost had forgotten she gave to all of us.

During that time, Mahin and I were equals. We were equals in grief. We were equals in tragedy. We were equals in concern for our parents. It was the first time in a long time that I witnessed my older sister not as a rebel but as one concerned for my parents and me. Perhaps she knew that and seized upon it on the last day before she was to go back to finish her studies in America.

"Shideh, there has been so much to share in this awful, unthinkable tragedy. We now must fully understand the extreme nature of the Shah, his government, and minions who created this monstrous murder."

I had to let her speak. For this time, it was not an ad hominem diatribe directed at my 'naïve' parents and me, but rather a seemingly genuine discussion of a person who knows that extreme forces created this massacre and we cannot distance ourselves from it. Still, I questioned it.

Mahin, how can we blame the Shah? "I heard the man from Father's school tell him quietly the other night, 'Hamid, I detest the Shah, but my friend from the police force tells me these murders have the fingerprints of religious extremists on them'."

"This will be spoken, Shideh, but I know for a good fact that the SAVAK was behind this…this was another way to show how brutal they can and will be in the face of opposition to them."

"But Mahin, I know we search for an answer, and you speak from the heart…but isn't Abadan a place not like Tehran, but rather of simple, working people and perhaps workers, technical professors, not philosophers or politicians from the university?"

"Shideh, whatever you want to believe, our nation believes this was another signature Shah atrocity…I know this from the people I am working with in America…you will know this when you go there, and people like you and me will lead the way for freedom and justice for our nation, even from outside the nation."

I was not sure what Mahin meant that night, 'leading the way from outside'.

But more importantly, I knew who most of the country thought were the perpetrators. In our own home, pictures of Queen Farah, which I remembered being in the house since my childhood, had been not only removed from our house, but I saw them in the flowered wastebasket Mother always used.

Chapter 12
No Guns Here

As the leaves changed their colors that fall, Ruth Holmes, always impeccably dressed, always stately looking in appearance, seemed to be graying in pallor. The Holmes split-level home never was without people coming in and out, mostly in the form of Erin and Maggie's friends and their kind and social neighbors. It might appear to an outsider that efforts were made to prevent Ruth from feeling any inclinations of loneliness, but it was really the natural flow of the hometown atmosphere that existed in the late seventies in the cozy hamlet of Eastwood.

Right before the holidays, Erin received her 'Early-decision' notification of acceptance to Georgetown University. At their annual family Christmas party at Uncle Ryan and Aunt May's, a few too many drinks compelled Ryan to slip out a previously well-kept secret.

"Well, can everybody join in? I want to make sure we toast three important things—the life and memory of my brother Ted, the acceptance to Georgetown of our beautiful niece Erin, and the passing of my nephew's gun training and license."

"Gun license?" Ruth exclaimed, shouting out in horror.

"Oh, my fault…not something I should be celebrating at Christmas…it's just a safety valve for Richard," the embarrassed uncle answered.

"A whaat? You told me Richard was more or less a mall cop. Since when do mall cops need guns?" The shocked Ruth answered.

Making matters worse, Ryan's imbibement of liquor clearly had diminished any discernment or logic, appealing, "Ruth, we're teaching Richard a lot of things, and chances are he'll never have to use it…"

"Chances? I lost a husband, and I don't now need to lose a son…Richard, you need to continue your college education now. I'm not losing you to a groomer for the F.B.I."

Trying to calm her mom unsuccessfully, Erin pleaded, "Mom, not now. Let's just enjoy Christmas."

"Richard, stay if you must…girls get in the car…May, Ryan, Merry Christmas."

Richard ran out the door, jumped in the front seat, and attempted to assuage his mother. "Mom, I'm driving you home, and I plan to get back to college, but I felt I just might need a little protection for you. Well, you know now that you're alone."

"Don't tell me you keep that in our house!"

"Mom, I'm sorry, but yes, it's in the locked safe on my bedroom closet shelf."

"I want it out. O-U-T, or you O-U-T."

Maggie and Erin were crying now in the backseat.

"Your father would never want you working with your uncle, carrying a gun…"

"Mom, I'm not carrying a gun."

"I should never have let you stop out of college…Richard, you were at the top of your high school class. This is my fault…this is my fault…"

"Mom, it's not your fault…things have changed for all of us…we didn't know all this was going to happen."

Pulling into their driveway, all four of them in tears, Ruth sobbed, "I cannot and will not let your father's death suck you into my depression. I will not."

Silently chilled by the bitter cold, the four walked up the path to their overly decorated home. Ruth, the last one in, stood on the brick steps and pulled Richard toward her. Flurries flirting on her aristocratic nose, she demanded, "You are my son, not my caretaker…you will finish your college education."

Richard, understanding the moment's intensity, assured his upset mother, "Mom, I never intended to do anything but."

Chapter 13
Be Radiant

Even the aroma of Grandmother Mashid's 'kohresht karafs', always soothing to the palate, and, more importantly, the soul, could not suppress our anger and grief, even past the forty days of mourning. We would be receiving no truth from the Gendarmerie or any facet of law enforcement. The information minister claimed it to be the 'acts of anti-government fanatics'. The newspaper Sobhe Emruz ran an editorial, 'Don't let us disclose who was really behind the Cinema Rex fire'. Almost immediately after our mourning period, 100,000 people took to the streets of Tehran, literally filling one side of the street to the other of our city. Days before, people had passed out pamphlets placing the blame on the Shah. Demonstrators shouted out, "Mekosham, Mekosham, aan keh baradaram kosht. I will kill whoever killed my brother."

Upon finding out about the tragedy, Georgetown University sent my family a beautiful letter of condolence. The letter read, 'The university will work with any of your needs and understand and accommodate any delayed arrangements needed for your healing from this unspeakable tragedy'. It was upon reading that letter that Grandfather Rasool was inspired to give me advice. Initially stoic, Mother and Father had become zombie-like figures- devoid of expressing emotion—not leaving the house, not even talking much to each other. Mother insisted that she cook the meals, but she was a mere statue in the kitchen. When the neighbors stopped coming, it was I who did the cooking. I fully intended to stay home and postpone my international studies for at least a full year, but I dreaded being in such a sad milieu where the sense of death soaked the walls and my mother's tears draped her chador.

"Shideh, your mother asked that I speak to you. It is important I speak to you as a voice for all our grieving family. We know you feel compelled to stay with your grieving parents, but you must go forth with your future of opportunity."

"Grandfather, how could I live with myself to leave at such a time?"

"Shideh, the mourning period has ended; life must go on. You must honor the memory of Esteri and become the best human being you can become. That American university writes with words of heartfelt compassion and love. This is a place where you will be able to bring your Persian heritage and, be proud and embrace the larger world. I must tell you this was in a dream I had—you are called to be the bright, enduring torch for our family, our culture."

"A torch," exclaimed Shideh, laughing, "Grandfather, are you serious?"

"Yes, a torch. Hatred and lies are smothering our streets, cities, and country right now. There is no telling if you don't embrace this opportunity now that you perhaps might be forever smothered by this turmoil, not even able to leave the country. You know we have a simple saying—*The dogs bark, but the caravan goes on*—You must be the torch leading the caravan of the best of us."

Grandfather Rasool, who I had known as the most humorous man I had ever met, was now the wisest. He was the wisdom that I needed in this time of grief for my parents, but I could not expect to get wisdom or any emotion from them in their deep well of sorrow.

A few weeks later, I would say goodbye to my parents and my neighbors. My mother, as expected, could not leave the house. Holding a bag of Persian Rosewater and cardamon muffins for me to take with me, she hugged me in an embrace I had never felt before. Father would drive me in his Paykan, chugging its way to Mehrabad Airport, the clutter of acrid smoke and explosive noise behind us, the Alborz Mountains in the distance, almost as bright as they stood in Esteri's painting. Dropping me off, Father could not muster more than a French expression I heard him say to me when I was very young, "Shideh, *Etre radieux*. Be radiant."

Chapter 14
Not an Ordinary College Experience

Richard went back to Villanova that spring semester all the time intent on leaving the school after the year. He found that being in a place where every guy, other than those on the international athletic teams, looked like they were born on the 18th hole of an elite country club was stultifying. Healthy enough to jog lightly, he assumed that he would soon be able to resume serious training and be back on the team competing. A meeting with the coaches directed him otherwise. The coaching staff insisted on his 'red-shirting' the full year. Coach Pyrah told him, "You can run the workouts with the team when you're able, but we don't want you going near a Villanova jersey until you're at full racing strength, and that's next year the earliest." Hearing that, Richard even considered leaving the school right then, but having promised his mother 'he would go back and finish the spring term', he stayed. His new roommate at Stanford Hall, Harold Anderson, was the bright spot in his semester. Anderson was a transfer student from The University of Maryland, Baltimore County. He was smart, funny, laid back, and fast. He had run in the low 47-second range for 400 meters, and the coaches were frothing at the trough of their track for the day Harold's required transfer sit-out period was over. It was a roommate friendship made in heaven.

One day, Richard received a call from his uncle Ryan telling him he would be on business in the area and 'would love to take him out to lunch, dinner, whatever was best for him'. His security business was expanding in Pennsylvania and Maryland, and they were receiving contract surveillance work from law enforcement agencies.

On a frigid winter evening at Kelly's, a favorite watering hole right off the Villanova campus on the 'Main Line', Ryan Holmes filled a hungry college student with good tap beer, so-so burgers, and an offer of excitement, something which was missing from his current humdrum school routine.

"Rich, I got your letter telling me you weren't going to be on the team. You just have to be patient and trust things will work out well."

"Yeah, I know, but I really miss the excitement and adventure of competing."

"Well, I got something that might help with that, but first of all, I want you to know that I personally promised your mom that everything was my fault, and I promised her that I would like you to continue to work with me in some fashion but without a firearm."

"What did she say to that?"

"Rich, that's part of the reason I'm here—she was okay with it. She told me that you were always a great 'saver', and she wanted you to keep those responsible habits to earn your own money…she is very proud of you, as we all are. I don't think I'm speaking out of school here to tell you that she showed me the beautiful cards you sent to her and your sisters."

"So, Rich, I have something exciting that goes beyond a mall cop status, but if you do as I say, you will find it to be not only adventurous but quite important."

"Sounds like really the thing I need right now, Uncle Ryan."

"Good. First, I have to give you a little background."

"When I was in the Bureau, I was involved with a very successful surveillance and watchdog group called COINTELPRO. We infiltrated subversive radicalized groups like the Klan, the Panther Party, the SDS, Communists, and other anarchists. Honestly, that's when I sort of drifted away from being your close uncle."

"Why was that, Uncle Ryan?"

"Well, Rich, good question. In every group dynamic, there exists someone—or more than just someone—who goes beyond the envelope. Consequently, within that group, we had seasoned agents who did what they were supposed to do, but we also had seasoned Bureau agents who just went off the deep end."

"What do you mean 'off the deep end'?"

"They, we say, 'bullied by badge'. They harassed witnesses, used unnecessary physical force, and made false arrests. Don't get me wrong, most of us followed the intent of the program—to identify and deal legally with any threats to national security emanating from those groups…but the program was exposed, mainly because of those loose cannon assholes. You know your dad was a pretty conservative guy, but, well, he spoke his mind to me when I let him know I was involved with the program. After it went public that some things went awry, he said, 'You better separate yourself from those reprobates…Do you guys know if it's the F.B.I. or the other guys who should be watched'?"

"Really, Dad said that?"

"Yeah, he told me I was getting like the British before the American Revolution. He always loved to use that expression as his catchphrase to portray an oppressive culture…maybe he used this one too many times."

"I think I know what you mean, Uncle Ryan."

"So, Richard, when I started this agency of mine, I wanted it to be modeled after the very best of the Bureau's intentions and practices, without engaging in any resemblance of illegal methods or practices…it is, after all, my name on the agency."

"Here's why I'm telling you all this. There is a case that I was involved with at the Bureau that I have first-hand knowledge of the criminal and criminals involved. It's a case that is very sensitive not only to myself but also to my partner, George Shea. It involves the murder of New Jersey State Trooper Werner Foerster. He was shot and killed in a traffic stop. Not only was he a Vietnam vet who came home in one piece with his shit together, but he was also a great kid—strong, friendly, and dedicated. He had a wife and son who must be almost a teenager by now. George tears up every time the case is brought up and has seen plenty of tough ones."

"Did they get the killers?"

"Yes, after a manhunt, there was a shoot-out on the Jersey Turnpike, and the culprits were taken in. The main perpetrator of the murder was a woman, Joanne Chesimard, who had a laundry list of indictments for bank robberies, attempted murders, and even the kidnapping of a Brooklyn bartender, all of which she was acquitted. It almost seems she had more acquittals than charges—untouchable. But they finally tried and convicted her on this one just two years ago."

"So, she's behind bars?"

"Yes, but her group, the Black Liberation Army, is intent on getting her out, and they have a vast network not only in Jersey, but we have intel that they are all over in Philadelphia and Pennsylvania; we want to know where they are at all times we can. They are not planning a bake sale."

"Wow. I can't believe that stuff is going on right around us, and I don't have a clue."

"Well, Rich, some of my old buds at the Bureau asked me to help out on this. All they want us to do is to pass information up the chain. I don't need or want any credit for any valuable info, and I told them I'll do this gratis. Rich, here's how you can help us and the larger community at hand, and it won't be gratis for you. You think you can recruit your roommate, Harold, to join us to get paid for a little surveillance work?"

"Harold, you know about Harold?"

"Yes, your mother spoke highly of him; she said she and your sisters found him funny and a real gentleman. When you took him up home last weekend, he has a valuable asset in all this."

"What's that?"

"He's African-American. If you can get him involved, our plan would be just to have you guys go to some bars in some areas of Philly to try to identify some people. It wouldn't be anything more than that!"

"Uncle Ryan, are there bars in Philly where a White guy and a Black guy could hang out and not seem suspicious, seriously?"

"Richard, that's the challenge, but we have a car for you and some pay. If you feel you can get your friend and both, you can do it…"

"A car?"

"Yeah, it's a write-off for us…and think of it as the Christmas present I, unfortunately, was never able to give you. After all, a young man has to have wheels at your age!"

Chapter 15
Friend in a Foreign Land

The flight to America seemed so long. I wanted to read, but I could not. While I thought of Mother and Father, I was flushed with thoughts of Esteri, envisioning her joining me in some great adventure someday. Her promise of 'giving me strength in my journey' rang true as when I thought of her, I could feel a tug of renewed confidence in my travels.

Arriving in Washington, D.C., I was greeted at Dulles Airport by two students from 'The Students Serving Students Organization', Heather and Roger. The air outside was much colder than I anticipated, but as the first Americans I met, they were so very warm. They made me feel so at ease. They seemed so respectful and patient in dealing with my less-than-perfect English. Heather was sweet and quite talkative. I'm quite sure I never saw a person as white as she. She had big brown 'freckles' and was also a nursing student. She told me that she came from Boston, Massachusetts, and 'could have gone to a lot of other schools, but Georgetown is the best nursing school in our country…the mere idea that we do clinical in our first year of the program proves that'. They explained that if it was all right with me, they were going to take me to school via the scenic way—The George Washington Parkway.

I was surprised at how green it was for this time of year. As I looked out the window, I could see the Potomac River through the trees. We passed by one exit, and Roger said, "That is one exit you don't want to get off of. It's the C.I.A. property." We, of course, had heard of the C.I.A. and American collaborations on both sides back home, the Shah's and the opposition, but I ignored reacting to his comment. I came here for education, and I wanted to be as far from politics and anything related to it, as much as possible. Roger dropped Heather and me off at the Campus Housing Building.

At the housing office, I soon found out there would be no housing available for me on campus.

The woman told me, "Not to worry, we have arranged off-campus housing for you and several other students for ten dollars a night." I was getting a government allotment for four hundred dollars a month, so I knew I must be careful with the remaining one hundred dollars. I was assured my tuition was paid for before I left. Father complimented me on my industriousness before I left because I visited the Ministry of Education office six times to make this certain before I departed Iran.

Heather told me that there was a 'Welcome New Students' gathering at the student center and that after I settled in, she would 'come back and go with me'. I asked her if there would be food there as I was very hungry from the long trip.

"There is going to be so much food—and they are good at understanding to have all types of food—meat, vegetables, international breads, and drinks."

It was heartwarming to have Heather as my first 'hostess'. I knew she was trying to make me feel comfortable. At that moment, I wanted to tell Mahin and Aunt Mastoureh how welcoming and kind the Americans seemed, contrary to how ill they used to speak of them.

Two hours later, I might have had another opinion of that.

After the gathering, Heather told me she was going to take me to a great Georgetown attraction, 'The Tombs'. What I understood as the English translation of this word made me confused.

"Is this an American custom, Heather?"

"Well, no, just a Georgetown one."

"Will I need better clothing?"

"No, a matter of fact, you might be over-dressed."

Seeing the perplexity in the veins of my face, Heather announced, "Oh, this is a bar…a restaurant."

"Heather, I do not drink alcohol."

"No worries, I go there all the time, and believe it or not, I drink diet coke…I just go to meet people."

Roger was one of the first people we saw as we descended the stairs in this noisy, smelly room. He had a table for us with four other students. Heather went to get 'beverages for us', and I was left alone with five American males.

"You must really hate the Shah and his oppressive government?" Roger sputtered to me as he downed his yellow beverage.

I didn't know how to answer that, but I didn't have to, as Peter, a blond boy across from me, shouted, "You got it wrong, Rog; she probably loves the Shah. He is the reason Iranians have the ability to come to colleges for America, right Shi—how do you say your name again?"

"Shideh."

"Yeah, aren't I right?" He kept rambling without interruption, "Don't you remember Jimmy Carter went there a year ago and toasted the Shah and said, 'Iran is an island of stability'."

"Yeah, go ahead and use Jimmy Carter as an example, the worst American president ever…"

"Frank's right, Pete, nobody trusts Carter…plus he toasted the Shah with champagne on national Iranian television."

"So what's so bad about that, Roger? He was showing American diplomacy."

"Peter, it's a Muslim country—alcohol. It is supposed to be taboo, you idiot."

At that, the four boys turned their heads apologetically toward me. Fortunately, at that moment, Heather came back with our beverages. She understood my look. It was the unspoken international language we women could understand. Calmly, Heather said, "Good night, guys…we'll see you on campus."

I knew I had a strong friend in Heather.

Chapter 16
Security Test

"What's this, Blaze?"

"Ah, it's a car genius?"

"No, that's not a car; that's a Ford Crowne Victoria LTD…in the hood, we would say that screams 'cop mobile'."

"Well, that's my uncle's Christmas gift to me, and that's our wheels from here on in."

"Okay, I take it your uncle is doing pretty well. That's one Christmas gift that costs a pretty good coin…"

"I guess this new private security agency of his is really taking off."

"Richard, serious? What would he be doing getting his smartass college nephew and his roommate to do some spy work or whatever the hell you got me into doing…no disrespect, but I'm sure he's got some sweet arrangements with his cop friends into shaking down drug dealers for a little extra pocket cash?"

"Ok, Harold, when you call me Richard, I know you're serious…so I'm gonna get serious now—my Pops and my uncle are the two most honest guys I have ever met…it's like a family thing—my dad told me once his father told him, 'I don't care whatever you become, whatever you do, as long as you do it honestly. You can be a garbageman as long as you're hard-working, honest'."

"Blaze, we got to cut this shit—my old man was a garbageman; he had no choice but to be honest, but I get your point. I meant no disrespect…but are we really going to do this thing tomorrow?"

"If you're in, of course."

Ryan Holme's plan for Richard and Harold was for them to casually go to three bars in North Philadelphia which have been designated as hangouts for friends of the BLA. Holmes had supplied Richard with pictures of men and

women, 'spots' to identify, or what he told him unequivocally, 'I&D'—
Identify and dash.

Twenty minutes into nursing warm bottles of Rolling Rock at Chet's, an antiquated dive off North Broad Street, the two became leery of two tall African-American men who occasionally made it a point to stare, or so it seemed, in their direction.

"Uh, Blaze…I think it's time to blaze our asses out of here before we get a serious ass-kicking."

"Okay, but did you get a good look at them?"

"Yeah, enough to tell you they are tall and look like me…I don't know about you, but I'm getting the hell out of here…it's time, I believe, to 'I and D', as your uncle instructed."

Getting out of the bar relatively fast, the two new rookie adventurers howled as they drove back on the Schuylkill Expressway.

Laughing, Richard said, "I'm not sure if we accomplished anything, but it was kind of fun."

"Yeah, sure, Blaze…that's why your skivvies have more skid marks than the Schuylkill…better slow it down; we don't have no stinking badges, you know, and they don't call it the 'Surekill' for nothing."

As promised, a seemingly inquisitive uncle Ryan called two days later.

"How did it go, Rich?"

"Honestly, I'm not sure, but we did mark two big tall guys eyeballing us at that Chet's place."

"Rich, I want to be the first to tell you; you passed the spy test."

"Whaat. I did?"

"Yes, you recruited a valuable asset in Harold, and you identified two unfriendly…by the way, those two guys work for me, two ex-detectives from Brooklyn Narcotics…"

"The two tall black guys…if they work for you, why were they in there when we were?"

"Richard, I had to give you some backup support on your first OP."

"My first what?"

"Well, your first adventure, we'll put it…but they said you guys handled yourselves like pros. I think you were right last week. It's probably better. Harold works alone in some of these places…hey, did he like the car?"

"Uncle Ryan, am I out?"

"No, you'll drive Harold. We want him to join a BLA student association over at Temple…could be really intriguing…we have very good information that they are passing on some heavy stuff to the student members there."

"Heavy stuff…what do you mean by that?"

"Just speak to Harold and see if he's good for this."

"Uncle Ryan…keep in mind we are still college guys…student-athletes, you know…"

"Rich, I never forget what you're down there for, but as legit college students, you can really help us out here."

Chapter 17
A Quick Study of Language

"Sorry, Shideh, that Roger and those guys were such dicks last night."

"What is this 'dicks'?"

"Oh, you know, idiots, rude people, jerks."

"You mean like *shetan*, Heather?"

"I guess what is that?"

"You know—the pooh, the waste material…"

"Ha, ha, Shideh, I get it—*shetan*…I'll keep it in mind when I need to quietly curse somebody out."

"I'm worried, Heather—our Shah and Queen Farah have now left the country, which might not be a bad thing, but there is so much looting and chaos now over there, I'm not sure what will happen. My mother is still so upset about my sister's death. My father and others were arrested last week for demonstrating against the government's lack of providing information to victim's families of the perpetrators of the *Cinema Rex* massacre."

"Was he detained?"

"No, fortunately, my aunt Mastoureh finally did something good for us and helped to get him out. Mother says crowds of people were chanting for hours, 'Shah raft—the Shah is gone'. But, I fear, will whoever replaces him be better—this we do not know?"

"Shideh, if you don't have him as a professor, which you probably won't this year, I want you to meet one of my professors here—Professor Jan Karski. He is a fabulous man, and he actually survived the Katyn Forest massacre in Poland and later escaped a Nazi P.O.W. camp. When he teaches, we know this man has witnessed human suffering and atrocities and is very good to speak with."

"It would be good to speak with him. Thank you, Heather, for this suggestion."

"He might be at the orientation tonight. You will love him if you get to meet him."

"Heather, so many meetings and socials, will I be ready for my classes?"

"Yes of course; but, remember this is Georgetown, and we study hard and socialize well and often…hey, as somebody in the 'Students Serving Students' organization, I get to introduce you to the president of the university—Father Tim Healy."

"Does he really want to meet with me? There are so many students here."

"Yes, he does…when I first came here, I was a little intimidated by the Jesuits, but they are really great men—they are smart and low-key. Father Healy is a big champion of our international students and of building bridges through education."

Later that evening, we dined and met more people and students. It was good to finally meet some other students in my nursing program. But Heather was right, the man who gave the welcome speech, the president, Fr. Timothy Healy, came over to a group of students and myself. He was quite pleasant and asked us where we were all from. He said something I would never forget. He told us, "If you get what you expect here, transfer at the end of the year. If you get what your parents expected, transfer immediately."

We had to wait as some students had their translators and wanted the correct translation. Father Healy went on to say, "Your dream is your job. Pursue it against all odds. You have the great gift of youth among you. For us, we live in the regret of dreams unfulfilled and in the spirit of your dreams." Although we were full of smiles, the meaning of those words needed to be digested, prompting almost awkward silence. Soon enough, they were perhaps the most important words we would hear in all the languages listening to them.

My classes were at once challenging and interesting; however, I knew I was in the place I wanted to be in when the Dean of the Nursing school told us in her opening remarks, "Georgetown nurses don't work at hospitals; they run hospitals." I thought of the words Grandfather Rasool told me, "Many are besieged with trouble with others; besiege yourself with healing for others—that is who you are." Mother told me how much turbulence there now was in Tehran, 'worse than ever'. I was convinced that peace would always be a constant in my field. I wanted no politics in my life, only love.

One night at the very end of the month, Roger came chasing me while coming out of the Lauinger Library. I was exhausted from both my clinical and my classes. Out of breath, he exclaimed, "Shideh, I haven't seen you in a long time...the student radio station, WGBT, is closing down in a couple of days...they ran out of funding money. But I told them about you, and they want to do an interview with you about the impending return of Ayatollah Khomeini. Can you do it? It'll be great."

"Roger, tell them they are dicks." I didn't see Roger for a long time after that.

Chapter 18
Somebody Intriguing

"Richard, I'm going to do that Temple thing…and then I'm done. I can use the extra cash, and it sounds easy, but that's it, man. I have too much going on—our training is getting serious!"

"I kind of intimated that to my uncle, and you got my wheels whatever you do—I can't do any more of this if I work with my uncle again, it will have to be in the summer if at all, these business management courses are hammering me."

Harold found that the Temple meetings were 'tame' and 'full of rhetoric', but he was led to a significant meeting at a small women's college outside of Philadelphia. The most compelling information he came across was his meeting and conversation with a Cuban-American from Florida named 'Raul'. Harold asked him what brought him from Florida to Philadelphia. Staring with dagger-like eyes, Raul answered, "Libertad." Raul proceeded to ask Harold where he was from and why he was there. Thinking fast, Harold answered, "I'm from New York?"

"What borough? I spend a lot of time up there in all the boroughs, you know, man, I hang my hat in el barrio…lots to score there, mi Hermano?"

"Well, I'm there as a student at NYU. I'm really from down South."

Realizing he was possibly about to get cornered, Harold found a way to grab a granola bar from the table and make his way out. Exiting, it appeared that Raul was following him out. Harold was correct in parking the Crown Victoria outside of campus with its 'clergy' sign sitting prominently on the dashboard. Nervous and knowing the jeopardy he would be in if his identity were ever found, he hid behind a school bus, checking if he had room to flee. Harold sprinted to the car, feeling safe enough to get out of there unnoticed. Halfway through his dash to the car, he turned back and noticed a figure moving and stopping. It was clear it was Raul who gave up on any sort of chase. He quickly realized he was clearly outmatched by, unknown to him, a star college sprinter. Immediately, Harold looked forward to telling Richard that he successfully sprinted what was probably his first 800 meter. What Harold didn't know at the time was that the information and identification of 'Raul' would be the most valuable information he passed on to Ryan Holmes, who subsequently passed it on to the F.B.I.

All he knew was what he told Richard back at Stanford Hall. "Rich, these are some serious bad asses…I think we are out of our league…I'm solid; how about you?"

"Harold, like I told you, I'm done for now. My uncle is going to have to get some full-time old cops or gangsters for this stuff."

Richard and Harold went back to being regular college students, at least until the semester ended and summer break began.

Mason's Island, Connecticut

Richard's friend Lou was the hero of the summer as the promised stay at his friend's family's place on Mason Island came to fruition. The trip to the tiny bucolic island off the coast of Eastern Connecticut was a year late but not any less special. Harold blended perfectly with a bunch of old track guys who marveled at his times and stories of his races. Tommy Gaffak managed to get three of the guys in his Carmen Ghia, and it was no problem for Richard to get the rest of the old teammates in his Crowne Victoria. There was one catch. When they finally arrived around 10:00 pm that Friday night pulling up on the dirt road with only the light of the Long Island Sound illuminating them, it appeared that no one was home at the rustic bungalow. Apparently, Lou miscommunicated on the weekends. His friend, now his girlfriend, was nowhere to be found.

Harold, the last one out of the back of Tommy's Carmen Ghia, surveyed the scene and wailed out, "Well, Uncle Ryan taught Blaze and I every house has its weakness."

Only Tommy would be sharp enough to ask the obvious question, "How does Harold know your uncle Ryan?"

Richard was quick to reply, "It's a track metaphor he heard from me…" The answer was good enough to prompt the boys not to have their planned adventurous weekend thwarted by a small miscommunication or a locked-up summer bungalow. Searching around, the boys did find an open screen window, pushed it in, and in half an hour, had their sleeping bags pulled out and were soon fast asleep. The weekend couldn't have been better—sailing on the catamaran they found on their phantom host's property across the street, drinking, running, playing volleyball on the side yard, and more drinking. Richard imbibed in the taste of a summer of fun and innocence, one that he would never forget.

Washington, D.C.

With summer winding down, Erin had to report to Georgetown for her freshman orientation the third week of August. The Crowne Victoria was packed to the gills with Erin's clothes for the semester, Maggie's three bags for the stayover, and one knapsack of Richard's. Heather was once again acting as a welcoming host for 'The Students Serving Students' for the incoming students. She recruited new help in the form of Shideh, whose English was getting better by the week. Richard nearly ran over the curb when the Holmes pulled up to Healy Hall. He had his eyes fixed on one beautiful dark-complexioned woman with a multi-colored scarf around her. On the drive down, he insisted that he 'would help with the heavy bags'…"but Mom, you have to do everything else as I have to get in a long run on the towpath everybody talks about."

Uncharacteristically, Richard missed his run. Carrying Erin's belongings back and forth, he listened as the cheery Heather plied Erin with information on nursing school and how the girl with the beautiful smile and Mideastern accent asked Erin and Maggie about themselves. She turned to Richard, "It is nice to have a brother." Richard wanted to say something, anything, but he was at a loss for words. Maggie asked Shideh where she was from. "Iran."

"Cool, we've never met someone from there."

Sensing something she had never observed in her older brother, Maggie whispered to Erin, "I think Richard really likes her."

Chapter 19
College and Home Conflict

By the end of the semester, I was receiving no communication from the Ministry of Education in Iran. It was imperative that I should receive information on my tuition payments. Another Iranian student I had met on campus, Gulshan, explained to me that her family insisted she end her studies in America and come back to 'continue her education in our great university in Tehran'. This clashed with the rumors that the new regime was closing the universities. Often, I awoke at night with the thoughts of my F1 Visa being pulled and my dreams shattered.

One day, when I explained my worries to my clinical professor, she responded, "I have the perfect solution. Due to your high grades, you have qualified for a teaching assistant position." This came as a complete shock to me, and due to her serious nature, I only later realized this was an incredible act of benevolence accorded me. Mother and Father insisted that I not return home at this time. Unsure of the security of the government allowance I had been receiving, I continued to accept the money my mother and father would still send me. However, I knew this was too much of a burden on them. One day, Heather offered me a suggestion for money. Heather's father had owned several ice cream places in the Maryland-D.C area, and she insisted that his one location in D.C. needed a responsible person working, maybe even managing it...and he would want to pay 'off the books'.

"What is this off-the-books mean?" I answered embarrassingly.

"It means cash—so you don't have to worry about being taxed."

"Will the government be alerted to this?"

"Shideh, I mean no disrespect...this is summer work...you are in America...our government has enough problems than to police hard-working students violating their Visa statuses."

Heather was the angel who welcomed me to this new place and was always there whenever I doubted my journey. It was almost like she could read my feelings the way Esteri would. While she was assigned as my 'Preceptor' at school, my nursing mentor, she was so much more. Without her, I could not have survived the early morning bus rides to my clinicals. She taught me a great trick—'If you are ever worried about the 5:00 am wake-up call, wear your scrubs to bed…you just get up and go'.

My main concern now for my 'new job' was if I would know the flavors well enough, as it had been a long time since father would take Mahin, Esteri, and myself to have *Bastani-e-nooni,* saffron ice cream, our favorite, or any other ice cream on Pahlavi Blvd. The stand, the Boulevard, and my sister would remind me of my young, innocent life. Those places and a person were now wiped away forever from forces I could still not comprehend. For now, I was a recipient of a constancy of love and concern in a small window, a window that might be shattered in my far-away home, but one which exists in certain hearts of people, whatever complexion they have, wherever they are, or where they might be from.

My calls home became increasingly more disturbing. Mother particularly always would start out a conversation feigning joy, but eventually, she couldn't help herself, telling a tale of the latest story about a neighbor who lay victim to the 'new, changed regime'. Mrs. Rastami, whose daughter I grew up with, was arrested by the Komiteh, morality police, sent to the horrible Evin Prison for 'not properly covering herself two blocks from her home'. In one conversation I'll never forget, Mother spoke of the strangeness of 'passing mullahs on the street cavorting with men who smelled of alcohol, and seemed to be carrying food during this time of Ramadan…many people act openly like markhor, wild goats'. She commented in perhaps the most ironic of conversations, "Even your aunt Mastoureh has been at a loss for words." I could tell in my mother and father's voices what they had said and what they had not said that they wanted to leave. But the rumors of *mamnoo-ol-khorooj,* the prevention of leaving the country, were alive, and nobody seemed to want to run sideways of the new regime.

One day, midway through the fall semester, I became fully aware of how, despite the thousands of miles of distance from my country I was, the chaos and confusion was still close. My friend Ayesha, a Persian girl whose family had left Iran in 1975 to live in France and who was enrolled as a student at

George Washington University, walked with me from her business classes to go off-campus down to her 'favorite sandwich place, The Booeymonger Deli'. As we walked through the gates, there was a group of about two dozen 'student' demonstrators with signs 'American Incubates a Murderer' and 'Death to the Shah'.

Ayesha would receive copies of the Iranian newspaper *Kayhan*, and even from that pro-regime paper alone, one could read about the daily turbulence in Tehran and elsewhere. Mother would refer to 'how friendly the clerics were, always asking me for you and Mahin'. Father would now speak of them in glowing terms. It was the acceptance of frightening things. I imagined this to be a survival tactic. Ayesha expressed that her parents spoke in the same fashion. She insisted it was because the new regime was 'bugging' all international calls.

'students'. "My father always said that student demonstrations were a 'rite of passage' during the Shah's rule and reign, but it seems they are now more seething than ever." She implored me to look at the group and see if I recognized any actual students from campus.

"Do you see anybody that you might ever see in classes or on campus?"

Quickly glancing with a look certainly not thorough enough, I just demurred, "No."

"You won't—because most of them are from elsewhere—with one exception."

Pulling my elbow as we crossed the street, Ayesha nodded her head in the direction of a boyish-looking man wearing a brown denim jacket with ripped blue jeans.

"Look closely—he is the shaytan, troublemaker. He is Abdalbari Ghorbani, and he is the leader of the 'Confederation of Iranian Students'. I'm surprised he or his group haven't approached you."

"Well, that's one of the benefits of being up the hill. Most people here don't know we nursing students exist...did he approach you?"

He actually did...his first sentence turned me away totally...he said, 'You should be with us of your own kind'. "I walked away from him, telling him, 'You're definitely not my own kind'. Maybe I'm too much of my father's daughter, but he did warn me not to get involved with any Iranian political group. He said, 'You are in college for an education, and the student groups never get what they are demanding anyway'."

"My friend Fatimeh, who's at GWU, goes to the meetings and tells me that she doesn't like all that they talk about, but Ghorbani promised her he would get her and others to Lebanon this summer and that the trip would cost them nothing."

"Lebanon?"

"Yes, something about an Islamic cultural tour."

As we walked, I could not help but think about the last student I knew who traveled to Lebanon. We really never did know the nature of Mahin's trip there. The worst thoughts were now circulating in my mind.

Chapter 20
Worth Pursuing

The fall semester began, and Richard and Harold went in for an off-campus housing suite on a side street off Montgomery Avenue. Two teammates, Paul Benson, a Long Islander, and Fred Dunleavy, whose Boston accent was as thick as his sense of humor, went in on it.

"Richard, this is our year—we are e-l-i-g-i-b-l-e. Eligible. Put it out there. Give me five."

"Yeah, yeah, it should be good."

"Should be good…should be good…this is coming from the guy who got my sorry ass out of bed to run freaking five miles around that island in Connecticut. Seriously…what's with this bullshit 'should be good'?"

"No, I'm psyched…I've just been thinking about a lot of stuff lately."

"Oh no, don't let your head play games with you, my man. You will be ready to compete, it might take a few months, but you will get there…"

"It's not that…it's not about running…I guess I didn't realize how much I got…how good I've had it…hell, did you see that picture last week in TIME magazine of those eleven guys getting shot point blank by an execution squad in Iran?"

"Iran…what the frick?"

"Yeah, it's chaos over there…it was supposed to be better when they got rid of that Shah guy…but I've been reading…people are getting executed left and right over there…the major cities are starting to look like one big ghetto."

"What a minute, Rich…since you brought it up…news alert…same shit, different country…you don't get it, even the best of you white folk don't get it… ain't no different than where I'm from in the good old USA, a new politician promises new things… better change… less crime… more opportunity… NOTHING changes…I started running because I had to book away from the scary-ass drug dealers five blocks from my apartment building…they're still there for real. Iran? Please. Rich, you know I never knew your dad, but I can tell from your family, and you know I love your family, that he was a great man, but man, your dad not alive, well, the truth is your family is still better off than my family with my dad alive…brother no disrespect but don't give me no sob story about Iran."

At that moment, Paul came. "Whad da fuck are youse guys having a hissy fit about…?"

"Freddy, yo…you better check this out. Ozzie and Harriet are having a spat."

"What's this about…it's got to be about a girl—Blaze tells Harold and Paul about the foreign chic at Georgetown."

"What…Richard, what foreign chic…this is news to me?"

"Nobody."

"Hey, Rich…and I'm not going to call you Dick…"

"Nobody ever has, Paul."

"Well, why don't youse not be a dick then and tell Harold and me what you told Freddy D about the foreign chic…we're your family now?"

"Harold, I knew this was not a good idea…"

"Ok, I'm gonna guess—is this girl from Iran?"

"Well, yeah, but I don't even know her. I just kind of gazed at her…you know she's different'."

"Oh, this Love Boat stuff is killing me…just get laid and say good night."

"Paul, just fuck off will you, and everybody will be happy!"

"Yeah…I am gonna fuck off to the keg party…youse guys continue your soap opera…Fred, ya coming?"

"Rich, I'm sorry, you want to talk now that the Einstein Brothers are out of here?"

"Well, I don't know why I even bothered to tell Fred, but when I dropped off Erin at school last year, she was there on the student welcoming committee. She was stunning. It just seemed she had it all together. She had a mad nice name, Shideh, and I already looked it up—it means radiant, and Harold, no shit, she is radiant!"

"So…you got her number, and all I take it?"

"No, I didn't really speak to her."

"I don't know, the pink and green girls around here don't do much for me, and I mean, I dug those blue-eyed, blonde, voluptuous Jersey Shore lifeguards and all, but this girl just hit something in me…and it was only over the course of minutes."

"So now you're studying the history of the country she comes from?"

"Harold…well, yes, but I can't believe all this stuff that has been going on over there, and I had no clue, no clue, and we thought we were like international spies when we sat in a couple of bars identifying some local gangsters."

"Rich, not to burst your bubble, but remember your uncle told us spotting that dude Raul was bigger than we want to know…and he also told us that we are probably the only college kids in America doing that shit."

"Yeah, I guess we got it going on."

"Hey, Rich, you know I'm down if you need somebody to travel down to D.C. to visit Erin."

"Thanks, Harold. We'll be doing that for sure."

Chapter 21
The Despair and Strength of a Family

As late as October, rumors swirled around about a 'great retaliation' against Mexico for harboring the exiled Shah, the United States, and any other country who aided him. While my homeland was thousands of miles from my doorstep, I was embraced in the grips of all of its turmoil. In early November, everything seemed to turn upside down when several hundred students our age took over the American embassy in Tehran. At the time, the gravity of the situation paled compared to the news I was about to receive.

Awakened by my housemate, Gloria, at 6:00 am, I knew this was not a clinical day as I checked to see if I had my scrubs on. "There is a telephone call for you...I think it is your mother, and she is saying something about 'Maman...Shideh...Maman'." Picking up the pay phone over our housing plywood wall, Mother was, in hysterics. "Uncle Ebrahim has taken his life."

Leaving Abadan's literal and horrifying heat, preoccupied with the tragic memory of death and resettling in Tehran, Uncle Ebrahim could never forgive himself for the death of Esteri, Somaya, and his wife, my aunt Nazarin. Mother and Father would have tea with him once or twice a week, but it was not a good grieving group. In his apartment off what used to be named Roosevelt Blvd., Ebrahim often spoke about 'retaliation' and bombing a government outlet, but it was Father who convinced him that that action would never bring back our precious daughter, niece, and sister-in-law. In a perverse way, Ebrahim's expression of regret and remorse in inviting the girls to Abadan allowed some solace for my parents. In any phone conversation I had with Mother, she would inevitably bring up Esteri and her rhetorical self-flagellating question, "Why, oh why, did we send her to that horrible place?" She, however, got over her hysterics soon enough. She made it a point to tell me that since, "Uncle Ebrahim hung himself with a copy of the Quran in his pants pocket, he was allowed to be buried in the Behesht-e-Zahra cemetery." I knew why she was telling me that. It was a bitter reminder that Esteri, Somaya, and Nazaran had no cemetery to be buried in.

For the next few weeks, the news of the hostage crisis barraged us. By the stories we heard from our parents of this emboldened and even more brutal regime, we knew that a brazen attack somewhere was coming. Ayesha told me that Ghorbani had approached her again after the hostage takeover, imploring, "Now won't you join us...can't you see there is nothing the American imperialists can do...they got Carter on his knees." When she saw Fatimeh, Fatimeh said she could not speak to her or anyone outside the student association anymore...there were too many important things going on...Ayesha told me, "Fatimeh has drunk the Kool-Aid," a phrase now chillingly too popular, derived from another mass following of a misguided 'protector'.

My sense of self was expanding to a degree I was almost unprepared for. One day walking to meet Heather for dinner, a Saudi student, walking with two American students, turned directly to me and called out, "Ya Kalb." Arab for 'you dog'.

It was my first experience being verbally harassed anywhere. It would not be the last. More than ever, I wanted to wear my veil, and I wanted my Iranian identity to be known so that if someone took the time to speak to me, they would know my Iran was not the Iran of the hooligans or the hostage takers. The American news stations were reporting the hostage crisis as a 'student takeover of the American embassy'. To live in Iran was to know that things were not always what they appeared. I recalled witnessing the 'student protests' with Esteri at Tehran University and laughing at the older men dressed as students, a sure sign that they were SAVAK infiltrators. It was clear that the new 'revolutionary' regime had learned from the Shah's henchman, and now they were going to be better and more ruthless at their own duplicitous tactics.

I, of course, worried where Mahin was in all of this. We had gotten close again after Esteri's death, and I longed for that normalcy from her, but her heart was in a much deeper place. A much darker place, I was soon to find out. She was my sister, and I could only love her if not understand her. We were always so different, but I knew she was a fighter. When I was nine or ten, in a neighborhood game of 'Catch the Handkerchief', a boy, one of the mullah's sons, accused me of getting out of the proper line. I wanted to reason with him, yet he pushed me. Mahin came and boldly pushed this thuggish boy to the ground. He got up and ran away. All the children cheered. I realized at an early age that with Mahin, I had the protective nature of a big brother and the friendship of a big sister. Something was gnawing at me that her protective fighting nature was somewhere being exploited.

Chapter 22
The Good, the Bad and the Ugly

"Rich, Uncle Ry here. I got bad news for civil society but good news for you and Harold."

"Uncle Ryan, this is a good time for us—we qualified for the regionals, finally freaking did it!"

"Great. Well, my news is almost just as good. Tell Harold that his intel on that Raul was incredible. 'Assata Shakur', which is what Joanne Chesimard, the murderer, is going by, was sprung out of the Jersey prison by some assholes in a well-orchestrated plot. Thank God, they didn't kill the correction officers; those poor guys were really shaken up, but the officers clearly identified one of the perps as a light-skinned guy around 6'2 the others referred to as 'Raul'. It is he—his real name is Diego Batista, a Castroite with an arm's length Miami rap sheet. Figures a Cuban Communist by the name of Batista would have had his name changed."

"Whoa, do they feel they can track these guys down? That's totally a police-F.B.I. deal, right? You don't need us now for anything, do you, Uncle Ryan?"

"No, Rich, just tell Harold it was huge information he passed on. The stuff he heard Raul telling the hippie girl at that college that he 'likes where he's living now except for the smog and smoke' narrows it down to three cities we think he could be referring to and where they're going to take Chesimard-Pittsburgh, Cleveland, or Los Angeles."

"Where do you think they'd go, Uncle Ryan?"

"Considering they and their dirt-bag troublemakers have been floating around the northeast for the last several years despite their arrests and trials, I say Pittsburgh…but apparently, I'm outnumbered by the agency guys. They all insist it's Los Angeles. They are going to have a watch group out there with warrants and everything…that's all the information I could get from them."

"What do you mean, all the information…"

"Well, I'm getting the impression from my inside sources at the agency that the new director, Bill Webster, who is a great guy and former judge, wants to tone down the reliance on any intel coming in from outside the agency. The fear is that would just create an outside type of COINTELPRO, and nobody wants to go back to that."

"Sounds about right from what you told me…understandable…I'll tell Harold. You know, Uncle Ryan, that money you sent him, he doesn't keep a dime for himself; he sends it right to his mom in Baltimore."

"Rich, you lucked out; he is better than a good roommate—he's an A+ good human being."

"No doubt about that."

"By the way, Rich, we got codenames for you just in case we have to transcribe anything we receive in the way of information from you…'Fleet foot A' for Harold and 'Fleet foot B' for you."

"I guess I'm long past being the Blaze."

No, actually…that's it—we can't use it—The Bergen Record just mentioned you using that moniker in an article on 'Local College Athletes Doing Well'. "Good luck at regionals and I hope to see you at Thanksgiving…by the way, I know you college guys don't have time to tune into the world news…but there's crazy shit going on over in the Mideast. Did you hear about it!"

"You mean the hostage crisis, right, Uncle Ryan?"

"Yeah, crazier than ever that Iran…of course, the government never learns."

"Which government, ours or theirs?"

"Ours, Rich, ours. They should have learned from the mistakes supporting the fascistic tyrant Batista in Cuba…the Shah was not much better—very similar, and now, just like Cuba, you have the inevitable revolution orchestrated by the brutalized citizens. In this stuff, you always end up with a really demented guy leading the country, worse than the first! This Khomeini is executing daily in public firing squads not only former generals of the Shah but regular people who aren't kissing his…he even put the former Prime

Minister, Hoyveda, through a sham trial and executed him last spring…sorry, I got off on a tangent.”

“No, that’s cool, Uncle Ryan. I thought I was listening to my dad.”

“What? Why do you say that?”

“It’s the first time, Uncle Ryan, I heard you question our government’s policies.”

“Rich, hey, I got a little carried away. Don’t quote me now…it’s bad for business, ha.”

“Don’t worry here at Villanova; not many students other than Harold and I seem to be talking yet about the hostage crisis.”

“Well, I’m glad you’re tuned in to the world as it is good, bad, ugly.”

“Yeah, I figured it’s about time I get tuned into that…good night, Uncle Ryan.”

“Good night, Rich.”

Chapter 23
Genuine American Invitation

I kept close to Ayesha, sharing whatever news we could get out of Tehran. Since my first-year credits at Ferdowsi were accepted in my transfer, I was considered a second-year student at Georgetown. We would spend weekends feasting on ramen and anything we could assemble over the prior weeks from the cafeteria in our pockets. This would be our lot for the coming holidays, I assumed as well. I cherished our time together, the two of us, longing to be free and independent, yet often alienated among the sea of American students.

Calling back home, I felt more than ever that my parents were inmates in their own neighborhood, city, and country. When my father made his second sycophantic comment about the mullahs, the sheer ridiculousness of my parent's current behavior revived a memory of a favorite parable father would say, even against my mother's wishes. "No one has ever seen the eye of an ant, the feet of a snake, or the charity of a mullah." I quickly recalled a story when neighbors were over at our house over the summer. Our relatives with the greatest Western antipathy, Uncle Massaud and Aunt Mastoureh, had left, and someone brought up the rumor of Khomeini's coming out of exile in France. Father blurted out a joke, a bold one, but not an arcane joke at the time. "If you lift up Khomeini's beard, you will see 'Made in England'." Everybody present laughed and laughed. My phone conversations now told me that no one was laughing anymore. I knew more than ever I could not return there until things had reformed.

In early November, everything seemed to turn upside down when several hundred students our age and even younger took over the American embassy in Tehran. This feeling grew stronger as the mood became more vehemently anti-Iranian and politically charged on campus. After a couple of weeks into the American embassy hostage-taking, tempers flared among many individuals.

One day while meeting Erin and other students for lunch at the New South Dining Hall, I witnessed an argument between five students, two Americans, and three foreigners.

One of them I recognized as demonstrating outside the gates with Ghorbani, the leader of the Confederation of Iranian Students, the week before. The stabbing verbal epithets they threw at each other were disgusting and hateful. Erin seemed disturbed and embarrassed for me. I asked if it might be better for us to take our sandwiches outside. While it was easy for me to stay 'up on the hill' at St. Mary's School of Nursing, away from the lower main campus, I realized I had really been sequestered from the strong feelings of many of the students down below. Walking back to an anatomy seminar, to my surprise, the ebullient blonde who had welcomed me on my very first day in America asked me a question that changed everything.

"Shideh, what do you do for Thanksgiving?"

Erin looked more embarrassed than earlier at what my answer might be.

"Why do you ask?" I implored.

"Well, my family would like to welcome you to come to New Jersey and spend it with us unless you have other plans, of course."

"I would love to be with your family for your holiday if it is not an inconvenience. Thank you."

Soon, I would never be so happy about not thinking straight.

The American holiday, Thanksgiving, and our spring holiday, Nowruz, or New Year, are very much alike. Although held at different times of the year, both holidays are celebrated in no small way and are significantly centered around family. I knew this, and I understood and appreciated the meaningfulness in this invitation from this tall blond Erin, whom I hardly really knew outside our classes.

Chapter 24
Attraction

"Richard, I just wanted to let you know your sister is bringing home a guest from school to stay with us for Thanksgiving."

"Heather, her mentor?"

"No, it's a girl from another country who Erin says is really nice?"

"Wait, it's not that Iranian girl who was with Heather when we dropped off Erin at school?"

"Yes, as a matter of fact, I think it might be…Heather has been now in a 'Preceptor' role for younger nursing students, and it seems your sister and this girl have had a lot of classes together and have become very close."

"Oh, okay, am I supposed to do anything?"

"Richard…we'll be having Grandma and Uncle Ryan and Aunt May as well…do you think you can pick Erin and her friend up at Penn Station on Wednesday? I don't want Erin and her guest to have to wait for trains to Eastwood?"

"Absolutely, Mom…I'll see you in a few days."

In his junior year at Villanova University, where he was a scholarship track athlete, Richard cut his last class on Tuesday afternoon and was home early that night. The next day, Richard drove into the city, not quite understanding why his heart was beating as it would before a race. The drive over The George Washington Bridge seemed interminable. He decided to park and walk to the Amtrak station. As he approached the platform, Erin and Shideh, in almost matching 'G' heather gray sweatshirts, were walking and talking in the manner of childhood friends. Reaching down in an effort to take Shideh's suitcase, he tripped and nearly fell. As the two girls laughed, Richard could not believe what he saw. This girl reminded him of a movie star, and her complexion seemed rich, smooth, more bronze than he remembered.

She seemed from another world when she spoke, "Richard, I actually packed lighter than I was going to; I hope that isn't too heavy."

Richard stammered, "No, I just was thinking about where I parked the car."

Suddenly remembering he didn't think to park in a garage but a side street, he said, "We have to make tracks to the car." The trio ran up the staircase, arriving not a minute too soon, as the car in front of them was attached to a towing truck. Although they escaped that hassle, they were awarded a one hundred dollar no parking zone ticket.

"This reminds me of my home city," Shideh said calmly.

When they arrived in Eastwood, there were messages from Tommy Gaffak and all Richard's friends saying that they were coming over that night. Across the hall, there was what looked like a fresh delivery of flowers. Knowing he meant to send flowers for his mother for Thanksgiving, but also knowing that he didn't, he looked at the card. It read, 'Thank you for your wonderful hospitality', and it was signed 'Shideh'. It struck Richard odd in a way he could not explain to himself that this girl had sent this to his family before she even arrived. He would find out later just how special the gesture truly was. Maggie came in and proclaimed, "I guess you're the happiest college guy around, now?"

"What's that supposed to mean?"

"Come on, Richard, Erin did this for you."

"I'm not sure what you're talking about, but Happy Thanksgiving."

"Okay, sure, but we hadn't seen you brighten up like you did when you saw her at Erin's drop-off since you won your last race in high school."

"Oh yeah, she seems nice."

That night, Gaffak and Richard's oldest schoolboy friends came over. They, too, were moved to silence when they were introduced to Shideh. Tommy made the token offer to ask Erin and her friend to join them to go out to a couple of bars in Westfield and Bergenfield, but Erin insisted they would take it easy that night, "Maybe tomorrow."

Driving into town, Billy Peterson couldn't help himself, "Blaze, Erin gets the sister of the year award for bringing home that girl…my sister brought home the gossip of the year; what planet did that girl come from?"

Mike Annuzio added, "That's no Jersey chic; she is from Hollywood or something."

Tommy Gaffak added, "Where is she from, Blaze? I'm guessing Saudi Arabia?"

Petterson, now they know it all, "Yeah, that's what I was going to say, or Egypt!"

"Actually, no, she's from Iran."

There was a long silence in the car.

Annuzio was the first to speak his mind.

"Iran…shouldn't you be careful…aren't we enemies with those guys?"

Gaffak, ever the most reasonable, chimed in, "Yeah, Mike, I suspect she's here to take Erin and Blaze's family hostage for a few months."

All the boys laughed and quickly were on to stories about their respective semesters. Still, Richard knew there would be even greater scrutiny with Uncle Ryan coming to Thanksgiving tomorrow, and it would probably be a good idea to hide or run out of beers around the house.

The next morning, Richard, just a few hours from being three sheets to the wind, won 'The Annual Eastwood Turkey Day Five Miler in the shade under twenty-five minutes'. Erin and Maggie persuaded Shideh to run the mile fun run with them, the first time in her life she had undertaken such an adventure. When Richard went up to the podium to accept the winning twenty-pound turkey, Erin walked with him and whispered something Heather had told her. Since Shideh had no credit card, she used her teacher's assistant's money to take a cab into Georgetown to a florist to send their family the flowers. It was clear that this girl was different than what he knew.

Thanksgiving dinner went better than Richard had assumed it would go. Uncle Ryan regaled everybody with stories about him and their dad growing up. Richard made sure he substituted the Heinekens for Bud Lites for Ryan. The mood turned somber but surprisingly sensitive when Aunt May asked Shideh about her family. Shideh briefly spoke about her parents and older sister, Mahin, but quietly changed the subject. Less than two years after losing their father, the Holmes family seemed to understand the sense of unforeseen absence and the void of lost or alienated loved ones this woman experienced, even if a world away.

Chapter 25
Choosing

As Erin and I rode back to school together on the Amtrak, my thoughts were vacillating from appreciation to apprehension about accepting this family's hospitality. Her family was so kind, her brother handsome and seemingly much more mature than the American boys I had met so far. Was I flirting with the well-intentioned American charitable culture, or was I the unique 'holiday ornament from a faraway place' that the Americans could tell their friends about? They were genuinely caring people, but I find myself doing what my friend Ayesha tells me, "Americans do too much of, and Iranians never do now-smiling." Ayesha had visited her cousins in Iran over the holiday break, and she told me that there was a highly noticeable difference between the two countries. Was I entitled to smile? I could only wonder what Mother and Father were feeling and how I so much missed them. The time I spent with this family was enjoyable, but I was growing increasingly restive as to who I really was. Was I an Iranian in exile, masquerading as a student, or was I a student in America temporarily disconnected from my true reality?

Ayesha told me, "Your parents are telling you a lie…they cannot be happy… the face of Tehran is now that of the mostazafeen or the downtrodden." If only I could be with Mother and Father and Mahin.

One day in the spring, President Carter sent a rescue operation into the Iranian desert to free the hostages. His mission failed, and American students were more hostile than ever to Iranian students. Ayesha contacted me…several students at George Washington University were beaten up, many of whom were of Mideastern descent but not Iranian. Ayesha was hysterical and asked if she could lodge with us 'just for a few days'. I met her on a Sunday evening by the John Carroll statue, having no idea she would be so bruised. For the first time in my life, I felt fear, shaken fear. I did not go to classes the next day, staying with her and putting icepacks on the bruised side of her cheekbone, which had been struck by a 'midwestern boy with a thick neck and anger spitting from his tongue'. She said that now, more than ever, she was going to stick with Ghorbani's group. When she mentioned 'going to Lebanon again', my thoughts ran wild as this perhaps was a way to contact Mahin. She pleaded with me to come to the Confederation meeting. I could not say no.

By Tuesday night, Ayesha's swelling had all but disappeared. She walked me down the canal path, up above the traffic horns of 'M St.', blurring into the night. The peacefulness of the Potomac to our right calmed my initial fright of walking in the DC darkness with another Iranian woman. We descended into the basement with what seemed like an even darker interior. Ghorbani was the first to greet us, "Salam, Haletoon chetor e Sarkur Khanum Shideh. Hello, how are you, honorable Shideh?"

Turning to a diminutive older man in mottled Farsi, Ghorbani said something about my sister, Mahin. I could not help myself and immediately said, "Bebakhsheed, Excuse me."

"I was telling my brother, Bijan, about Seyedah Elahiyeh, your dear sister, Mahin."

"You know her? What is that name you have given her?"

"It is an honorable name…we give a new name to all of our brothers and sisters of the revolution living abroad, to protect them from any imperialist bullies…and yes, we know your sister well from our pilgrimages to Lebanon…she is highly respected…we have been waiting for you to join us."

"I am here to help my friend, Ayesha, not yet to fight for the revolution; if you know my sister so well, tell me how I can contact her immediately."

"We can, of course, arrange that…but sooner or later, you will have to decide how much the path of the revolutionary struggle that your sister has chosen you will or will not embrace. Sarkur Khanum, the revolution will be here soon enough; you cannot hide in your studies."

Oddly, he gave me a contact in the Iranian embassy 'who had all the most current information on your sister's location'. I thanked him.

"Will you not stay for tea?" He asked. I told the truth that I had missed classes to be with Ayesha and must get back to my studies, but I told him a lie as I was leaving. I said, "Merci Agha Ghorbani Amma Bar migdaram! Ba'adan mibinamet. Thank you, Honorable Ghorbani. I will come back…see you later."

"Khoda Hafez. May God protect you." Ayesha felt obligated to stay; I felt no such obligation and would never return.

I hailed a taxi back to campus, knowing there were only two things for me to do now—complete my nursing studies and protect my sister from whatever she had gotten herself involved in.

Chapter 26
Chasing a Killer

Harold was flying through the spring, running roughshod on the oval at eastern collegiate meets. He posted a 45.8 relay split at the Penn Relays, bringing his 4x400 team from sixth to second. The following week, May's weather had turned unusually damp and cold. Harold was entered in the 100 and 200 as a 'tune-up' for the following week's league championship meet. Exploding out of the blocks in the 100 semis, Harold had a two-meter lead at the 60-meter mark. Seemingly out of nowhere, he catapulted what seemed an inordinate height upwards, grabbing his left leg. The whole trackside of the stadium went silent. His left hamstring, as was the rest of his promising season, was torn. The swelling seemed so intense as he was carried off the track; it was as if someone had painted a lavender swath across the belly of the hamstring.

It was debatable who was more crestfallen—Harold or his teammates. Richard spent the last couple of weeks of his junior year trying to keep his best friend's moods up, and his efforts were to naught. Harold Anderson's dream senior year came to an unexpected premature ending. However, a man with so many talents would not elude the aspirations of others.

"Blaze, I'll just cruise in the rest of my assignments for this end of the semester and probably take your uncle's offer to track that guy."

"What guy?"

"Wait, your uncle didn't tell you?"

"Tell me what?"

"Damn…I thought you knew—he's been calling me about this 'off the reservation op', he calls it—tracking this dude, a black dude, they know already is a bona fide terrorist. It involves a whole lot of cash for me if I file daily reports on his whereabouts and stuff…"

"I guess I'm out of the picture, Har."

"Blaze, it could be two things—this is too dangerous for your uncle to want his family involved, or there's no place for a pale white kid from New Jersey to fit it."

"Har—you're family—stop it…"

"No, Blaze, love ya—but that's what you don't get—I got responsibilities that you don't have, and I need the money."

"Ok, I get that, but whatever you need on the way of help, backup, whatever, I'm there."

"I think it's going to be me alone on this."

Ryan Holmes was salivating when his contacts from the F.B.I. gave him a 'priority client' for investigation. The agency knew the valuable information that his protégé' Harold Anderson had provided them in identifying the whereabouts of the notorious 'Raul'.

Both Washington police and the F.B.I. had thick files on a former Long Islander, now residing in the D.C. area, who looked like he was being groomed for domestic terrorism. David Theodore Belfield grew up in a modest Long Island home of hard-working parents, four brothers, and one sister. As an African-American, he had witnessed bouts of racism growing up in his community of Bay Shore. Enrolling at Howard University, he started to visit the Islamic Center, where he felt the teachings of Islam filled a void he felt as a minority living in a white-dominated country. He went further, changing his name to Daoud Salahuddin and embracing a radicalized view of the religion while dropping out after a semester at Howard. In November of 1979, he and a group of pro-Khomeini demonstrators chained themselves to the railings of the Statue of Liberty, holding a banner excoriating the Shah. One of those in the group was already known to be a belligerent radical by the name of Bahram Nahidian. The Bureau described him as one of 'Khomeini's American operatives'.

Prior to that, Salahuddian had met Said Ramadan. Ramadan, one of the founders of the Muslim Brotherhood, had been on a speaking tour of the United States. Salahuddin became quite close to Ramadan, calling him his 'spiritual advisor'. At one time, Ramadan had enjoyed mutually beneficial support from the United States in their anti-Communist efforts. By the seventies, it seemed clear to many in U.S. intelligence circles that Ramadan, considered by many in the Muslim world a 'humanitarian', was more interested in pushing a radicalized Islamic agenda. By the time Ramadan had met Salahuddin, he was encouraging Salahuddin's actions, even violent actions, in support of the Islamic revolution.

"The idea is for me to get close to this guy and attend Islamic Center meetings, your uncle even wants me to consider learning Arabic and Farsi to understand any conversations or any plans these guys might have."

"So I get your being a black guy might blend in with Mideastern guys at the meetings?"

"Blaze—this guy Salahuddin is black and American, and if you look at pictures—we have a strong resemblance; it's just crazy."

"Yeeeah, I guess I wouldn't blend in…when do you start?"

"Like right now…next week I have to go for training in Virginia…they were kind enough to let me go to my graduation."

"I don't get it—my uncle told me that COINTELPRO program was shut down…what's this about?"

"Richard, this is serious stuff; this isn't wiretapping people who think differently."

"Wow, when you call me Richard…I can't believe you actually just called me 'Richard'—you have drunk the Kool-Aid, Har."

"Shit, Blaze, no wonder your uncle told me to keep you out of the loop on this."

"I just hope I didn't get you into something that is more than some fun we can tell guys about."

"We aren't going to tell anybody about any of this."

Chapter 27
Mahin Appears

Ayesha came over, exclaiming, "I have the best news, even if it's from a source that is not pleasing to you. Your sister, Mahin, will be in Washington tomorrow."

"My sister…in D.C., how did you find this out?"

"Ghorbani…But through my friend Kaleh, who is going to his meetings…"

"No need to apologize, Ayesha, I'm numb. Why wouldn't my sister call me somehow first?"

"Maybe she wanted to surprise you, yes, maybe that's it…maybe it's a surprise."

"If it's tomorrow, I have required clinicals…I just don't know…it's always like this with Mahin. Everything is always so much in secret; everything is and always has been so nerve-wracking…I just wish Esteri was alive…I'm sorry, I just have these bad feelings when I know I should not."

"You are entitled to your feelings…perhaps your sister has feelings as yours to nursing as hers are to the cause of the revolution."

"Ayesha, what are you saying?"

"Well, I am reminded of my mother's old Persian saying, 'Every cook has his own way of making soup'."

"Ayesha, what words do you speak?"

"Shideh, you are my friend. You are beautiful in so many ways. You want to help people, so you came to a faraway place to be a nurse; you are honest, and you are to be believed in your every step. You are the bowl that is hotter than the soup. But oftentimes, I feel you separate yourself from your past."

"Ayesha, I am troubled. What are you saying?"

"Well, something I can never forget…when I was very young, my father was a lover of poetry and believed in things that my mother would tell him were 'from a world not to be thought of'. He loved poetry…I have heard you talk about how your father loved the poetry of Omar Khayyam, as we all did. My father's favorite poets were Khosro Golsorkhi and Forugh Farrokhzad. When they were both brutally killed by the Shah's SAVAK, Golsorkhi, executed after a sham trial, and Farrokhzad in a set-up car accident, my father grieved as if his children were killed. We vowed to hate the Shah after that. I remember that. The revolution has ended all that."

"Has it, Ayesha? I like you, want to believe this is true; I just don't know?"

"I'm just saying to listen to you sister, she loves you, she wants to see you, let her talk."

Seemingly looking for a way to minimize the time spent with her sister, Shideh, in a gentle blurt, looked Ayesha square in the eyes, saying, "I hope she understands I have a twelve-hour clinical tomorrow…"

Walking down the hill the next day, Shideh barely noticed a young woman walking toward her. The woman, wearing a white tee shirt and weathered blue jeans, blended in the cosmopolitan Georgetown summer heat. She could have easily passed for a well-tanned Italian-American young woman. Shideh looked up in a quick glance of affability, a token gesture in the community where she now had felt a comfortable part of. She would have strolled right by if it were not for the woman, in a loud but clear whisper, saying *Xvaharem* (my sister). The voice was unmistakable, and it was Mahin. Breaking down in tears, both girls embraced in a hug.

"Mahin…I am sooo happy…I am just confused…I heard you would be coming from my good friend, but I was not expecting here and now…"

"Shideh…can we go to your home? Perhaps a private place…my visit is an unfortunate short one…"

"A short one? You are here, my dear older sister. There is much to speak about. I want to reconnect."

"I have but mere hours in Washington…I have meetings in this region…but I do want to speak with you."

"If you cannot take the time to taxi with me to my place, we can sit in the place they took me in my first time to Washington—The Tombs restaurant."

"Is this place by a cemetery? Such the name?"

"I was puzzled as well by the translation in English, but it will be quiet now."

We sat down in the back. Mahin looked interminably uncomfortable. She appeared to look around several times a minute as if she were a fugitive being tracked down by hunters.

"Sister, why here? Why now? Where are you going?" I could not help but blurt out a few of the hundreds of questions I wanted and needed to ask Mahin.

"Shideh, everything that has happened to quell what happened to Esteri and others is now over…we must protect our people, our revolution, that we never go back to that—the monsters of the monarchy."

"So you are protecting that? With whom? It is my understanding that last year, they found, tried, and executed the perpetrators of the murderous fire. What about the kidnapping of the Americans? That seems to have made only enemies of this so-called revolution."

"Shideh, I can assure you that is just to show how we, as a small united nation, are not afraid of any superpower. I speak with my friend Niloufar regularly…you know her as 'Mary', the interpreter for our captives."

"Mahin, you have a script of answers for everything: the hostages, the fire…"

"Shideh, it is more than the fire. It is the fascist practice we must never let return to our country…Xvaharem, I am *khodi* (an insider), and I will be that for the revolution forever…we cannot let forces of the Great Satan enable our nation to go back to that."

I could not speak for what felt like a long minute. When my sister, whom I grew up with, whom I played on the street with, whom I laughed and watched episodes of *My Uncle Napoleon* with, uttered the words 'Great Satan', I stared blankly at her as she stared down at a now cold soup that I knew she was never going to sip upon. She knew I could not stomach this talk.

"Sister, when did it become the 'Great Satan' to you? When were you having your parties at UCLA, when you were sleeping with your fraternity boyfriends? When you were getting an education that few in our country could get? When Mahin, when?"

Mahin rarely had ever witnessed an outburst of rage like I spoke that day at her, and she was clearly troubled by it. She began to get up as if to give a speech to a congressional delegation.

"It is time, Shideh. You refuse to see the clock that exists not on your wrist but in the sky of suffering that so many people live day to day by."

Slapping down several dollars on the table so hard in the almost emptied restaurant that men on the barstools several meters away turned to look in our direction, she said firmly, "I will be with the revolution forever, will you?"

Mahin's tone was rhetorical. She walked hurriedly out of the restaurant, blowing a kiss in my direction. I screamed in her direction, "There is still much to speak about; we are not school children. I would like to see you again. Let me call you a cab."

Her pace quickened, walking away much faster—waving her right hand in what seemed like a gesture of 'thanks, but no thanks'. She seemed to be staring down at her wristwatch on her left hand, perhaps sensing the suffering of others all too close at hand, perhaps sensing the suffering I felt, that we were out of time as sisters.

Chapter 28
Proving His Worth

"Harold, you know my partner George Shea?"

"Well, this is the first time I've met him, but Rich has told me a lot about him."

"The pleasure is mine, and I wanted to thank you for helping us locate Chesimard's accomplices…she's still at large, but I'll go to my grave trying to bring her to justice for the murder of Werner, our brother."

"I want to echo that, Harold. This case is more immediate, possibly more dangerous, and that's why we had you go for that training in Virginia. We really appreciate you coming to Jersey here. The first and foremost thing is nobody, absolutely nobody, can know anything you are doing for us except the people in this room."

"Of course, Mr. Holmes, Ryan is the only one I have spoken to, and it actually slipped…"

Noticing the two men looking disapprovingly at each other, Harold chimed immediately,

"As I said, it slipped…"

Shea, breaking his façade of a cool, calm, collected individual, screeched out, veins piercing his pale Irish skin, "Nobody…absolutely nobody can know about this…look in the mirror tonight and repeat, I'm in this alone…at least ten times."

"Gotcha."

Shea caught himself and let Holmes chime in, Holmes taking a charitable tone.

"Well, I trust and love my nephew, but Harold, this has to be a solo deal…just the nature of the high-security issue. We are going to give you three numbers you are going to report back from on payphones. If you feel there is anybody questionable around you when you are making a call, use the code that has been given to you to abort the message."

"I can't emphasize enough how the information you attain we believe is critical to national security issues, and people at the highest levels want that information."

"There are, of course, some perks…outside is a graduation present—a car…"

"A car?"

"Yes…you are going to need that…one of my old friends I used to work with is a great and loyal member of the Hmong community down in the D.C. area…he owns a dealership in Silver Springs, and not only did he give us a great deal on it, but he has also created a special recording device that you can trigger, when and if you need to turn it on to record a conversation."

"Ok, I really appreciate the car, but I'm not quite sure why I'll need a recording device?"

"Harold, it's mere tradecraft. We have several strategies we want you to consider, and we need to go over them right now."

The air of immediacy was as thick as the veins in Shea's neck.

"We need you to join the Islamic Center. Your goal will be, by your third visit, to befriend, if not Salahuddin, at least somebody who appears to be in his confidence. You will want to invite them to go to a diner or a café, give them a ride. We're actually not sure if Salahuddin has his own vehicle—at least there is nothing registered in his name or any of his possible aliases."

"Give them a ride…aren't they going to question how a young brother has a car?"

"Harold, sorry, we didn't get you a Mercedes, we got you a used car—a Dodge Duster—it's still great, like we said, 'we got a good deal on it', there are bells and whistles in it, but only you know about them…your line is that it was your old man's car—something like he passed it on before he passed away…Geez, I'm sorry."

"That's alright, and I wouldn't expect any less of a crack coming from a cracker…"

With penetrating momentary silence, Harold burst out laughing, and the two would-be 'crackers' knew they had more than the right guy for the task.

"Perfect, Harold, just remember that 'crack' as you are ideally mimicking Salahuddin's universe…you have witnessed marginalization in your community as a man of color, and you are looking for answers from Allah…your college world was vanilla, and you wanted out…the white people never cared about you…if you have never felt hate…create it now and show it!"

At this point, looking out the Jersey window at a stormy cloud above the New York skyline, Harold felt comfortable enough to be himself.

"Solo deal…show hate…this is some serious shit you got me into."

"That's putting it mildly, Harold…the guys down in Virginia said you handled the sleep deprivation training, the car spinning drill, and all the other stuff like a veteran. The question is, do you feel totally in?"

The two men, looking that they would be better off on a shuffleboard court in south Florida, waited the interminable seconds for Harold's reply.

Chapter 29
The Blur of Music

I came home that evening in a cold sweat. The cup I was pouring tea into was shaking uncontrollably, or was it I that was shaking? The worn couch in the center room never looked so beautiful. I just wanted to dive into it and fall asleep and make sure I would end up in a dream place that was far away from this real place I found myself in. As I settled in, the phone rang. Could it be Mahin apologizing? No, I thought further, she would never apologize. That's one thing she could or would never do. She was the older sister and always thought she was in the right no matter what. It was beneath her. I put my head back down to rest. Within minutes, the phone rang again. I grabbed it with anger.

"Hello, Shideh? It's Erin."

I must have really confused Erin as it took me several moments to gather myself and answer her.

She spoke a little louder with a tone of concern.

"Shideh? Are you there? Are you all right? Did I get you at a good time?"

Hich chizi nist. "Oh, I'm sorry, I had been speaking with a Persian girlfriend…It's nothing I meant."

Erin's warm, friendly voice was the sun in the darkroom of my feelings. Within two minutes, I felt I was back in control of myself, and we were speaking as if we just left off that morning. She mentioned her brother was in town and wondered if I was free for dinner. Despite my emotional and physical fatigue, there was something inside me that told me it was the right thing to do to see them. Her brother seemed kind and handsome, and I needed a break from everything in nursing and my concern with Mahin.

The patience and understanding in Erin's voice cooled me in the heat of that summer evening. I sensed the perspiration dripping down from my back was cooling. While I felt a sense of calm, my anxieties over Mahin wouldn't abate. We all tried to put her Lebanon trips out of our minds. I heard only through neighborhood innuendo at home in Tehran that she was living a 'Wild American student's life at UCLA'. Then, all of a sudden, those rumors were gone, and she was the American student spending time in Lebanon. The fact couldn't be ignored anymore. My sister was an angry foreigner in America with political feelings that had overtaken her. That never seemed to bother me until now. There were a lot of those students and former ones, especially in D.C. I understood their passion and their need to vent as they were living now in a sea of freedoms that were taken for granted by the people who had known nothing else. But after a while, most had cooled in their envies and hatred of America and Americans. But for Mahin, those feelings seemed all the more visceral. Worse, it seemed like she was engulfed in a veil of preparation. I sensed she was preparing to be a part of something I could not even imagine. It seemed I knew my sister less than ever before.

I asked Erin only one request, not to eat at *The Tombs*, telling her I'd explain later. She responded by telling me that, of course, it would be fine, and she just wanted to get together. We decided to meet at *The Third Edition*.

Richard, standing outside the restaurant, wearing a black polo and jeans, was looking absolutely nervous. It was funny as I tried my best to look like the typical American girl as if that were important. The truth was, other than the white sundress and sandals I was wearing, I really had little else in my wardrobe to wear. Erin came out, and the three of us, at first, stared awkwardly at each other as if Erin was waiting for Richard to say something. Silly as it seems, I don't know what I was waiting to hear from him.

"Wow, Shideh, it's really great to see you."

I wasn't sure if he had a summer sunburn, as many Americans have this time of year, or if he was blushing, but his remark seemed very sincere. The restaurant was quiet but loud enough to fill in the pregnant pauses of conversation. It seemed right to be with them, but I sensed Erin was planning something else.

"Shideh, Heather, and her friends are in town and were wondering if you wanted to go to *The Cellar Door* later to hear somebody Heather says is really special?"

"I love to."

That idea seemed to put Richard at ease, and he started conversing more freely and openly.

My concerns about Mahin had drifted away, as did the hours of the night. The time in the evening was a blur, and even later, at *The Cellar Door,* we continued to talk over the music. It was so good to see Erin, Heather, and the friends she came with, but I was entranced by the devoted interest that Richard was showing me. It only occurred to me later that it had been many months that I had really thought about who or where I was from. That night, I was adrift in stories about my grandparents, Mashid and Rasool, my childhood pranks, my parents, and my bone-deep memories of Esteri. I was able to do all this because a few feet across the wooden floor, there was a pair of kindly eyes seemingly straining to hear every word I spoke. Patti Smith's strident voice was just a sound in the background.

Chapter 30
The OP

"I have read your first report; so glad you're on board, Harold. That was a very astute observation of some of the members of the center giving the right arm signal—we know that is the signal of the brotherhood of the Iranian Basiji, so it's clear there is infiltration of this peaceful center…we even have a name for this OP."

"OP? As in Operation?"

"Yes, Harold, you're in the big time. We are calling it Shore Bay."

"What am I going to do? Something involved with water?"

"No, no, it's the inverse of the town Belfield. I mean Salahuddin, I grew up on Long Island, Bay Shore."

"It's really easy to process that he is just an East Coast American kind of guy."

"Well, I read, Harold, where you've joined the Islamic Center and have made contact with him. Is there something you developed further?"

"I can feel the indoctrination process…not the prayer part of the meetings, that's kind of peaceful…it's the discussions afterward; I feel guilty for liking myself, my country."

"What about your relationship with Salahuddin…are you getting close to him?"

"Absolutely, he wants me to come with him to visit prison inmates…it's something he does. I'm down with that, did that with my church group back home. Crazy thing, he, like me, is a great sixties soul guy. He says he meditates sometimes with War's 'All Day Music' in the background. He actually has very eclectic soul music taste—He likes Martha Reeves and The Vandellas, The Spinners, The Shirelles, Junior Walker and…"

"Harold…Harold…Harold…that's just fucking great, but you do know we have reason to believe he is a potentially dangerous, homegrown domestic terrorist; you do remember that, don't you?"

"Mr. Holmes, I am just following my training at the Virginia center to 'get as close as you can to your target or asset'."

Catching himself and calming down, Holmes reiterated his happiness with Harold's progress. "Yes, true, you have done a great job, getting in, getting deep. Have you intercepted any contacts of his? Has he spoken about Ramadan and Narhidian? You seemed to have emphasized in your report something about a light-skinned woman, possibly Mideastern, you have seen him with after meetings wearing a chador?"

"Yeah, he speaks about Ramadan as if he is the second coming—he says he knows him better than his family or friends knew him…but something doesn't feel right about the woman. Three times I have seen her with a group of women in an old Pontiac after the meetings, but she is the only one who comes out of the car and speaks to him."

"Have you asked him about her…is she a girlfriend?"

"That's just it—he cleverly avoids any conversation about her—Wednesday, I was waiting to speak with him. It seemed he was having a conference with her, kept looking around and all. Finally, he came over and went right into analyzing the prayer meeting, telling me he wanted to hear more about me, totally crushing the chance to speak about the woman."

"Well, keep on that, but I know the guys inside reading your report with her mentioned just negated any interest in her."

"Oh, why is that?"

"They feel if she is somehow connected to the Iranians, they would never have a woman working for them in this country—it would just be too out in the open with a woman, especially wearing a traditional look?"

"Mr. Holmes, who's to say she wears it all the time? The glances I have taken of her are that she could pass for an Italian-American girl from Philly or Baltimore."

"Okay… good point—but for right now, stay and build deeper conversations with him, and yeah, maybe you can get him in your car and play some of your soul tapes and develop from there…can you get him in that car— the agency really wants recordings?"

Two days later, Harold, coming out of a deli on a hot July afternoon, was passed by a white male in his forties who did an abrupt U-turn, saying something clear enough for Harold to understand the message.

If anybody was paying attention, the male could have been made from miles away as an F.B.I. agent straight out of J. Edgar Hoover's playbook for his white open-collared shirt and robotic walk. His one sentence, "Hot day like this…you have to get an iced tea," was indeed an established code message. All Harold had to do was nod. That was the warning for Harold to speak with Ryan Holmes immediately.

Harold, calmly rushing to his car, made sure he drove at least two or three miles out of the neighborhood to find an available payphone.

"Harold, good. Listen, new directive. Your instincts were better than mine. The agency wants you to follow the woman."

"Whaat, do I ask why the sudden change?"

In a terse, ominous retort, Holmes demanded, "No. Whether or not the woman you spoke about is with Salahuddin, follow her. Do you hear me? Like white on rice, follow her. Apparently, she has a more radicalized background than our guy."

Chapter 31
Rising in Love

The night with Richard was the happiest I've felt since I came to the United States. He started to come down on weekends, always late on a Saturday. He explained to me how important running was to him, and on Sundays, we would drive to state parks in Virginia and Maryland, where he would run as I waited with a picnic. But we never did much picnicking, as when he came back, he would put on a dry tee shirt, and we walked and talked for hours. One day, he described the feeling and sense of freedom he gets when he runs. I thought this was ironic, as it reminded me of the same feelings I enjoyed as a child in the foothills of the Alborz Mountains with our family. The scents of wild mushrooms and rhubarb came back to me from those days. Through Richard, I was remembering what was special about my homeland.

His questions were always so kind in nature. He wanted to know about my father. I told him about my father's love for the outdoors and sports, although he was never really an athlete himself. It seemed as though my father wanted one of the three sisters to be more involved with sports.

Father often spoke of *Mahin Korechian*, a basketball star, as 'the greatest athlete in Iran'. We liked her because her name was that of our older sister. It was hard for me to speak about Mahin because she seemed so close, yet so far. There would be more time later, I felt, to speak about her. Richard accepted that she had been a foreign student like myself, who simply had a different experience than I did. Richard seemed to understand when he would say, 'California makes everyone different', as we would both laugh.

He was so interested in my stories of our culture. I regaled him with stories of *Nowruz and Bazaaris,* but most of all, my emotional memories of Esteri. He listened as I told him of our great poet, Hafiz; his tenderness warmed me, as did the poet's words. His eyes, wide and kind, put me in a place I had not been for a long time. I felt a rocket shoot me back to my homeland, my family, and our cherished date palm.

He explained to me that since the death of his father, he found himself 'less social with others', but he had a very good, trusted friend in Harold Anderson, whom he had become distanced of late since Harold had graduated a year earlier than he was to. My feelings grew strong for Richard, and I sensed his did as well for me. When we kissed that late August afternoon on top of High KnobTowers with the sun setting on our faces, I felt a passion that was not ordinary and would not remain ordinary.

There were pressing things for me at this time that transcended the momentary strong feelings I felt for Richard. I had to come to terms with what I was going to do, where I was going to nurse, where I was going to live.

Chapter 32
A Killer Gets Away

22 July 1980. Ryan Holmes couldn't reach Harold soon enough. When he finally did around 5:00 pm, Harold had just come back from a jog.

"He did it. Our fucking guy did it."

"Mr. Holmes, who? Did what?"

"Haven't you seen the news this afternoon…a former member of the Shah's embassy living in Bethesda was shot at the doorstep of his home in cold blood, three gunshots in the stomach this morning. His name was Ali Akbar Tabatabai, a former press aide for the Shah, and he was very much out in the open about opposing Khomeini—"

"And you guys are sure it was Davoud?"

"Agency knows it was Salahuddin…we have witnesses describing a black guy about 5'9 fleeing in a U.S. postal jeep which he stole…it was him. Shit, why did I order you off him…well, I know why—it was a directive from the agency. If anything was going to happen, we thought it would be at that Anti-Khomeini rally Tabatabai was organizing this weekend."

"Did we get him?"

"Not him, yet, but agency has a couple of accomplices in custody."

"Mr. Holmes…I have to say, I am shocked…I know Davoud sounded intensely bitter at racism and stuff in this country, but I didn't see him capable of actually killing somebody. I heard anti-American rhetoric but never any Iranian stuff."

"Harold, you have done good, but you are still a rube with these types of killers…geez a couple of days ago, a couple of them attempted to kill the former Prime Minister, Bakhtiar, once a Khomeini ally over in Paris…they have death squads, we still don't know if Salahuddin was a part of an Iranian death squad or acting on his own."

"F.B.I., C.I.A., every police force in this country is on notice tracking down Salahuddin."

"You said he stole a U.S. mail truck, and he had accomplices; the hit sounds very well-orchestrated."

"Well, it absolutely was, and every assassin has a handler."

"Mr. Holmes, are we? Am I still involved in this?"

"Harold, more than ever. Agency guys are on the search for him because it more than likely involves inter-state flight and dealing with inter-state agencies, and you still are a 'ghost', but the agency likes the woman. We want you to stay in Maryland and still meet and pray at the center and see if she or the group of women show up in any of those circles…dammit, we had him."

Two days later, Salahuddin was reported to have successfully fled the country, and Holmes told Harold he had to report immediately for a meeting with the F.B.I. In a three-hour 'debriefing', twenty minutes were actually spent extracting important information about Harold's time with Davoud and the Center. Two and a half hours were spent on Harold's understanding that his 'mission never existed…there will be too much blowback, and it can't be perceived that another COINTELPRO was going on'. If he were to hear the term 'Plausible Deniability' one more time, Harold felt like he was going to choke someone. The 'debriefing' felt more like an interrogation.

Walking out of Holmes' office after the F.B.I. had left, Harold turned to Ryan Holmes, "I'm sure the F.B.I. isn't always this scattered all over the place."

"Don't be so sure, this isn't the first clusterfuck."

"What does this mean for me, Mr. Holmes?"

"Well, truthfully, Harold, F.B.I. will distance themselves from our agency, but I'll have work for you…P.I. stuff and the like. But Harold, you were an ace. We both knew you would have gotten close enough to, if not prevent the killing, apprehend this fugitive. I feel you have better outfits to work for ahead in this game if you so choose."

Chapter 33
Burlington, Vermont

Mahin's letter postmarked from Montreal came days within the invitation to a 'Graduation party for my two favorite grads' from Mrs. Holmes. Mahin's letter, in its overt blandness, sounded frightening. She wrote, "I need to see you and shall do so through our friend." I did not know which friend she was referring to when this would be, yet I was terrified by its cryptic nature. There was no return address; however, I felt I, too, needed to see her. She would be forever my sister and my love for her would never waver no matter what trouble I feel she must be involved in.

The party could not have come at a better time as it helped me settle the complexities in my mind regarding Richard, my family, his family, and my future. Richard's mother was a soft woman with a sturdy physical presence. Her eyes echoed the warmth I felt I saw in Richard's eyes. Her devotion to her Christian faith mirrored my mother's Muslim faith. She had what she described as 'St. Brigid's Cross' adorning the center hall colonial house hallway. There were three statues of different forms of Mary, the mother of Jesus. She noticed my examination of one where Mary's eyes seemed to sparkle. She explained to me that Mary had always been there for her during her husband's last moments on earth, after her husband's death, 'always, always, always'. I longed for the day she could meet my mother—two angels on earth. Mrs. Holmes, who pleaded with me to call her 'Ruth', apologized to me about her satisfaction with Richard taking a job with the Mohawk Bank. She knew that he would rather be closer to Baltimore and my new position at Johns Hopkins Hospital, but 'it would be good for all of us to have him close again'. It was a soothing day and quite different from the unexpected familial 'gathering' that I was soon to experience.

I was enthralled yet initially nervous with my position in pediatric I.C.U. at Hopkins. It was something I longed for; it made the journey of my studies from Ferdowsi to Georgetown meaningful, the endless hours of clinicals, examinations, and observations, so worthwhile. By late fall, I felt comfortable in my daily undertakings. The suffering back home now took on a whole new dimension with the brutal invasion of my country by Iraq, and I knew that to embrace a life living to help with other's sufferings would make sense of the thousands of miles I existed from my nation's own suffering and carnage.

One early November evening, with the first chill in the air tusking at my tired cheeks and the few leaves adorning the hospital campus and splaying the crooked sidewalks of Baltimore, I sensed someone following me. Deliberately stopping to reach into my bag, for I know not what, a woman of Persian descent called my name.

"Shideh Joon, I am a friend...Mahin has sent me." Handing me an envelope, she told me that it was safe for me to see Mahin and 'There was something in there that would help'. Opening the envelope, I noticed there were several hundreds of dollars and a note. It was a note from Mahin in her handwriting I have known since childhood. It read, "I am safe and would like to meet you in Burlington, Vermont, next weekend if this is possible. If it is, please call this number and say 'Yes' when someone picks up, and I know you, my beloved sister, will be coming."

This was conciliatory for Mahin. I could not sleep that night, my heart trembling even the next few days in my rotations. Honoring Mahin's last request in the note, I did not tell anyone. It would be the first and last time I would be untrue to Richard. He had asked me to come to visit him, but I informed him that I was visiting my nursing friends from Georgetown.

I used the money to book a train ride to Burlington. It was the first time I was on Amtrak since my first Thanksgiving trip to Erin and Richard's. I was to find my way to a restaurant named Bove's. There was a sense of trepidation in my bones as I walked alone among a street of people who looked very different from the people of both Washington and Baltimore. I felt noticeably out of place where the only other women wore farmer's overalls, and the men all looked like hippies from the pictures Richard had once shown me of his cousin's trip to Woodstock a decade or so before. Walking into Bove's, I was immediately struck by this beautiful, dark woman with short, cropped hair. It was Mahin. There were two men at separate tables, wearing open black jackets, with the almost too clean-shaven appearance which told me they were somehow together, and it didn't take long for me to figure out that they were watching over Mahin, as some sort of guardians.

Mahin and I embraced. "My sister, you look well."

I could only muster, "As you do…the hair?"

It's a look only temporary…I can assure you. "Shideh, we are very different, but I value what you do and long to tell you all my truths."

"I can only tell you I came the four hours to learn that," I answered immediately.

"Good… you will like the tea here…you can even get it with rosewater…"

The look on her face, her steely eyes, her composed countenance, spoke to me that I was indeed going to get several years of truth from Mahin once and for all. It was that which frightened me most.

"Sister, when we were very young, and you and our precious sister and mother would go to sleep, Father would often stay up with me and speak. This you never knew. Father often would express how powerless he felt in his position, as a teacher, as a man of humble means, to some of the awful things he knew that were being perpetrated by Shah and his unholy minions."

"Shideh, do you remember your childhood friend, Darya Mir, and how her dear father, one of our father's teaching colleagues, died of a supposed car accident?"

"Yes, sadly, it was one of the earliest tragedies of our youth I remember."

It was no accident, Shideh…he was dragged out of his car and murdered by SAVAK agents because he had joked about the Shah in one of the classes he was teaching at the university…Father knew of this, and he couldn't even tell Mother.

One night, father felt comfortable enough to tell me that story…and reiterated his shame at being, in his words, 'powerless'. When I went on to America, I was determined to learn one thing—never to be powerless. "Fortunately, I had a great professor in my sophomore year who helped me with that goal. He introduced me to the great Mostafa Chamran at a meeting of the Muslim Students Association, which he founded. This man empowered me. Someday I would hope you can meet him. He, too, like you, was a brilliant student who came to America on a full academic scholarship to Texas A&M and then received his doctorate at Berkeley. He arranged for my summers in Lebanon, learning, witnessing, fighting against colonizers…"

"Stop." I could not help myself. "He was the man who was responsible for your unknown whereabouts those summers…?"

"Shideh, his wife, Ghadeh Jaber, and I worked alongside in forging the AMAL Movement…this was a movement, as it is known of Hope…it was the Mahroomeen…the movement of the disinherited…it was working our Shia heritage to help our displaced, our disenfranchised brethren and sisters."

"Mahin, what else have you been involved in…why have our last two meetings been shrouded in secrecy?"

"Shideh…the Shah's SAVAK killed students at Tabriz and hundreds more much like us at our own Jaleh Square…I was proud to be a part of the revolution…when our friends were at the American embassy, they found, among other revealing American documents…cables telling about the briberies of Shah's officials by the American corporations GE, Northrop, Boeing, and others—the Americans and the Shah lay in their bed together while millions of our countrymen knew not of their next meal."

"Mahin…I know of the evils of the monarchy…we all did…but while you are reminded of the stories you shared with Father regarding this…why do you think our mother worshipped the queen, Shahbanou…why?…I'll tell you why—she walked with the lepers…she helped the disadvantaged…she created libraries for children…impoverished and uneducated children around the country…she is a living reason why I work with children who suffer as well…"

"Shideh…in this, you are brainwashed…she is a myth—she is now in the dustbin of history…"

At this point, I could not wait any longer…bursting out, "No…your belief that these revolutionaries are better people, are bringing freedom to others, that is the myth—Are you Sepah? Tell me now, sister, are you?"

"I am, my beloved sister, I am."

Instantly, the two of us cried.

"Sister, I know only this…the Shah perhaps did evil…but there is news of a worse terrible evil being perpetrated now in our revolution for freedom…My dear friend Ayesha's uncle, a good man, a mere officer in the Army, was executed last month along with dozens, if not hundreds of men, who wore merely the uniform of the Shah but had the hearts of all our neighbors and countrymen…executed in a barbaric firing squad."

"Sister, this is the news the press of the West only wants you to read…not the liberation of the masses…"

"Why can't you liberate love among people—I read the *Kayhan* in the summer months, and they were actually listing the daily executions—this is not the culture of our nation, this is not the culture of our great poets Sohrab Sepehri, Hafiz, Khayyam, and the one you loved in grade school—Farrokhzad."

"As Mostafa would tell us the great Persian saying, 'Revolutions are not made with rosewater', my simple sister."

"Mahin, why is it so difficult to just communicate with Mother and Father?"

Looking at her watch and snapping her hands at the guardian men whom I was never introduced to, she answered firmly, "That is because we now fight another war against the Iraqi invaders…but we will prevail…"

"But can't we work for the promised reform and love the revolution promised for the future of our nation?"

Getting up and looking around again, she said, "Please walk with me. I must get going…our differences are many…it is said that she who has no ill future is troubled with good…there is much to come…not all pleasant…"

We barely finished our tea, got up, walked two blocks, turned left, rounded the corner, and the two men got in a parked hearse with Canadian plates. Before I had time even to ask the normal question, Mahin exclaimed, "Our next meeting, I will come to you…do not be alarmed…but this is how I must travel."

I thought I was dreaming…my sister shimmied herself into a wooden casket in the back of the hearse.

I could only muster, "Khuda Hafiz." That would be my last look at my sister for a number of years.

Chapter 34
Harold Rising

Richard had grown out of touch with Harold, who was working in management consulting in the D.C. area. Two and a half years into the banking business with Mohawk Savings and Loan provided Richard with two promotions, but he felt he was still a glorified teller.

His feelings were stronger than ever for Shideh. He traveled more frequently to Baltimore, craving a desire for permanency with her. Richard spoke about quitting his job and moving to the Baltimore area, only to have Shideh counter his thought with, "You must not leave where you are until you have a job first." He didn't know whether that was a rejection of him or she wanted more from the relationship.

One day, Harold Anderson called him at work. "Blaze…I have some work in New York, and since I'm driving, how about I swing over to Fort Lee, and we grab lunch?"

"Awesome…I want to hear about this management consulting gig."

"Oh yeah, I have a lot to tell you about this!"

Three days later, there stood Harold looking as fit as ever and scoping out Richard's work desk.

"The three-piece suit is what I have to get used to, but you do look impressive in it…"

"Yeah, I guess this is something you'll be wearing longer than I will."

"What—don't tell me all is not sweetness with management consulting…what's with the name anyway? I thought it was a parody of all our friends at Nova and their drinking…Booze what!"

Harold's laugh was one of the best things about him—it was contagious and endless.

"Very good, Blaze…I'll bring that back to work—it's Booz Allen Hamilton—you are obviously so wrapped up in your banking circles that you're oblivious to a prestigious consulting firm," Harold announced as he tugged on the lapels of his Italian suit.

"Can't say I have…but who are you actually consulting, anyway?"

Looking around, Harold's demeanor changed dramatically, his pronounced forehead assuming wrinkles with the resultant intensity I had known him by; only Harold could go from utter jocularity to sheer intensity.

"Blaze, I am just there on a loan—I'm working a cover…for…"

Looking around again, hailing a hesitant sigh—he whispered, "Langley!"

Not really gathering totally what he was saying, Richard muttered, "Is Langley another consulting firm?"

Looking at me as if I had forgotten his name, my name, and what we had in the past, he double-down on his resolute whispering, "Langley—the company—the C.I.A."

Richard was initially surprised himself at his being surprised. Perhaps because he was just happy to see Harold, perhaps because he had a vision of some James Bond movie where this conversation would be just a movie; *This could absolutely not be their reality,* he thought.

"Harold—where did this come from? If you're for real…I mean, no offense, but I thought you would have had it with any of this kind of stuff after that OP with the terrorist radical you were to be watching was really botched by your handlers at the F.B.I.…"

"Salahuddin…oh yeah, Davoud, dear old Davoud, he's safe and sound in Iran—he was their agent, after all. We could have had him, I know we could have had him and prevented his cold-blooded murder of Tabatabai…shit, it still bothers me…course, now we have intel that it was a woman, our belief a college student perhaps, who was harbored for months herself afterward in Montreal who paved the way for his escape. We'll get her…we'll get her real soon…but I digress."

"No, keep talking. I'm still sort of shell-shocked by this."

"Well, I do have to thank you and your uncle Ryan…by the way, he says hello."

"Uncle Ryan?"

"Yeah, I got to believe he was instrumental in connecting me with the company, and he was one of the references for my D.O.D. application."

"Still Harold, the fucking C.I.A.? Again, no offense, but even you used the word 'botched', not that you botched it, but you know what I mean—you were more than a part of that OP, as you say…"

"Well, Blaze, it seems with the C.I.A. that doesn't matter much—as long as you know the tradecraft, have some balls, put in your time, and if you want out in the field—pass the farm…that's where I'll be in a couple of months…I'm hoping I get through that…so I will have all the checked boxes…"

"So, if you do pass the farm…shit…do you know where you'll be?"

"Oh yeah—if I told you, I'd have to kill you." Now Harold was back to his contagious laughter.

"Seriously, Blaze…I'm allowed max four family members to know what and who I am really working for…and since you're family, and there is no way I can tell anyone in my family without the whole state of Maryland knowing what I do, I will let you in…I have already been language immersed in Portuguese?"

"You're going to spy in Lisbon?"

"Blaze…first of all…how quickly you forget…we don't spy…we gather information."

"Yeah, that was true when we were getting solid beer money in and around Philadelphia…but crap…the C.I.A. is for real stuff!"

"I'll be in Angola…the good news is there are a lot of Catholics over there, so maybe that Villanova Augustinian stuff we were indoctrinated with will help out. But it's unclear whether I'll be with an NGO or working as a State Dept. Dude…the marks are the badass Russians flirting and confusing the people of that country being mired in civil war…we have significant friends, though they won't mess with us—even the Russians don't want the Chevron oil platforms damaged!"

"Crap…that sounds wild-my most wild thing I get to witness now is when I allow the middle-aged ladies I manage at the bank to bring espresso with their Italian pastries on Wednesdays and Fridays."

"Blaze…there's an opening for a guy like you."

"Fat chance…"

"Hey, how's Miss World doing—you and Shideh still an item?"

"Yeah, I'm still the luckiest guy in the northeast—I'm trying to figure that out."

"Why, you ask?"

"Blaze, I know you and what she means to you."

"Imagine that—maybe you could get her to roll Iranian assets."

"Fuck you, Harold—she's like the Saint of Johns Hopkins, and she's doing what I'm not doing—making an impact somewhere."

"Easy, Blaze, I was joking…well, you do this—and you surely make an impact."

Chapter 35
Too Much Time on Our Hands

The image of Mahin shimmed up in a hearse to go who knows where was frightening, to say the least. As the mysterious men with my mysterious sister drove away, she barely muttered, "Khuda Hafiz." It would be some time before I would see her again.

With the cities of New Haven, New York, Newark, and Wilmington whizzing by on the train ride back to Baltimore, I contemplated how different Mahin's life and mine have been. Where would Esteri's life have brought her? Would her presence bring Mahin and me closer? Everyone wants to go back to his or her childhood, but my childhood was becoming more visible in my dreams at night. Boys who would be Etseri's classmates right now were getting killed by the hundreds in the terrible Iraqi invasion of my homeland. Here I was, giving my life of care to beautiful suffering children, but how could I not be of use to the suffering of those children and men of my homeland?

Richard was coming down in two weeks, and thoughts of his carefree, easy-going style would be something I would greatly need. On the autumn Friday evening, he arrived; I could hear the chugging of his old car coming down my cobblestone street. Richard's interior was a soul wrapped in 'wells of good rain', as the poet Hafiz wrote, and his interest was not in the exterior. He once told me that material things just didn't excite him; people and ideas do. It was at that moment I was beginning to really love him.

Pulling his car outside of my apartment, I was quite sure he was about four feet from the curb....running out of the vehicle, he was holding something in his hand.

"Shideh...wait until you see what I got us. Remember, I was too late buying the Van Halen tickets last summer at the Civic Center!"

"Yes..."

"Well, I have STYX tickets for us for next July. You always love their song, 'Too Much Time on Our Hands'. These guys' music is great, and they are showmen. You are going to love it."

We got in Richard's Chevy, put in his tape, and started singing, 'Too Much Time on Our Hands…Too Much Time on Our Hands'. For a minute, maybe two, that seemed so true.

Friday's joy was shattered Saturday morning when I received a telegram. 'Father ill…terrible blasts from war every night…please come home. Maman'.

I would no longer have to mull over where I was going and what I was going to do; I would be leaving as soon as possible. It was fitting Richard was there; he knew I had to go, he understood.

Chapter 36
Responsibility over Love

The first person Richard wanted to tell about Shideh's imminent departure was his sister Erin.

"What? I'm pissed she didn't tell me."

"I think you will be hearing from her real soon."

"Erin, what do I get her?"

"What do you mean, you're like twenty-two years old, and you're asking me that?"

"C'mon, I mean, it's not exactly like I've ever had somebody, I, well, you know, like a…"

"Rich, I'm sorry. We all know what she means to you. Did you tell her what she means to you…did you?"

"I didn't get the chance."

"What do you mean…you were down in Baltimore the whole weekend?"

"I don't know. The Styx tickets pumped me up; we were laughing and singing, and then on Saturday…it was like depressing…she received a telegram that her father was not well. I mean, I know it's her family…I don't know, the whole thing sucks…"

"What sucks? You're crazy about her, and I'm pretty sure in her way, she feels that about you, and you would do the same for your family. I hope."

"But it's more; she told me it's more. She feels that she has to get home to her country to help with the war wounded. The freaking Iraqi thing…it's like I couldn't go to her country with her if I wanted to."

"And you want to?"

"Hell, yeah! SI just wants to be where she is."

"I have an idea. I'll go with you this weekend to Englewood; I know where you can get her a beautiful heart necklace—just don't be cheap, Richard."

"I would never be cheap to Shideh."

"Oh geez! Mr. Romance all of a sudden."

The day came. It was for real. After five years in America, Shideh would be returning home to Iran. Like a lightning strike, Richard would realize there was something monumentally missing in his life. Never one to be able to fully express his feelings, he kept crumbling up letter after letter until he could only settle on a store-bought card with a Hallmark manufactured goodbye and his simple written words, "I cannot and will not ever forget you, please never forget me…of course you wouldn't dare, would you?"

"Richard, the necklace is beautiful."

Both of them were similarly lost for words as they headed for Newark Airport with the smog, the setting sun, and the sounds of the tractor-trailers surrounding them, overtaking their ability to elicit any sweetness.

After seeing Shideh off and gazing at the envelope for several minutes, he opened it. Shideh's words were more romantic, more loving than he would want to know at this time. She ended up with words from an Omar Kayham poem that she said her father loved to recite. Shideh often told him how her father loved the words of this ancient Persian poet.

Waste not your Hour, nor in the vain pursuit of This and That endeavor and
dispute;
Better, be jocund with the fruitful Grape
Then sadden after none, or bitter, Fruit.
Love always,
Shideh

He reflected on those words, imagining Shideh, eyes beaming straight into his soul, reciting them. He understood more clearly, he appreciated her more, and he knew what he felt about her was overcoming him.

It was not but a month later that Richard was called into the general office of his bank. Richard could only hope that this was a different meeting than the epic meeting his father had at his bank. That, as Uncle Ryan put it, 'set the fucking domino of events that put your dad in the grave'.

Shaking his hand, the tall Mr. Vliet, of a demonstrative voice, and equally demonstrative receding hairline, announced to Richard, "Congratulations, you have earned a wonderful promotion. We are merging with a bank in Boca

Raton, Florida, and we would like to promote you as the manager of that branch."

"I might add, Richard, you can't ask for a better time to go: winter. Think of it: no snow, no ice. I know you are single—girls, girls, girls! But you have earned this position. You would need to be ready to go in two weeks, and I know it's the Christmas holidays coming up, but…any questions?"

"Mr. Vliet…"

"Please, Rich, call me Mr. V."

Something in his calling him 'Rich' for the first time ever made it apparent to Richard that the bank needed him to take this position.

"Mr. V., I am honored by this offer, but can I get back to you?"

"Rich, this is not an offer. This is a promotion. You, my good man, are moving on up. As I said, the good weather, the gg…"

"I know the girls…sounds great, and I am honored…"

"Okay, consider it done."

It was not 'done' for Richard.

Chapter 37
Tehran, 1984

Although I had anticipated change, I never realized just how different everything would be. There came a change in my mother's dress and her appearance; she now wore the full burka. Another burka-clad woman, whose voice sounded only a faint memory of what I could recall, accompanied her. It was Aunt Mastoureh, somehow more welcoming, more kind in her affectionate greeting than I would ever expect her to be. Nevertheless, I found myself pulling my head veil to make sure I was properly embracing the correct submissive look so she would not rail that I was *Gharbzadegi* or 'Westoxified'.

The drive home to northern Tehran was a lot to take in itself. The intense eyes of Supreme Leader Ruhollah Khomeini were startling in their appearance on the multifarious banners adorning the corridor of roadway from the airport to the city. The city, in its chrysalis of the Shah era, where the over-orderliness masked a turbulent tremor among the people, now seemed overt in its starkness and pungent in its directness of being a sectarian state. Heart-wrenching as it was to see the murals of the martyred young boys who were dying on the front lines in this terrible war, it was all the more gut-wrenching to pass by a freshly painted crane with freshly executed bodies hanging. The contrasting image was nightmarish. We spoke not a word as we careened around the corner. I felt my mother's nausea as if I were in her womb.

So many of the roads now had changed names, causing confusion in my head as to what direction we were going. Pahlavi St., the main trafficked artery, was now Valiasr Street, and as Mother made sure to say, "To Father's delight, Eisenhower Avenue was now *Azadi*—Freedom Avenue."

He always detested Eisenhower and those who took down his hero, Mohammed Mossadegh.

The city came alive to my memory as we passed Alzahra University, founded and once named after Queen Farah Pahlavi. We pulled over to a food market on Shahrdari Street, where Aunt Mastoureh quickly bought avocados, pomegranates, and walnuts. Mother promising, "Tonight we will eat *Khoresh-e-Fesenjoon,* and the chicken will be stewed to perfection."

Finally, walking into our house, Esteri's painting of the Alborz Mountains stood staring at my heart. I knew I was home.

Getting used to wearing the chador once again, I took it off once inside. I went to the bedroom where Father lay. His color was ashen, but his smile was both warm and strong.

"You are more beautiful than ever, my daughter…my wish is complete."

"It is my wish to walk you into our meal and hear your voice and maybe some poetry, perhaps good jokes, Father."

"I feel the time for joking has passed me, Shideh…tell me about America; the last time you were home was too much a time for sadness, but now we can at least be joyful in each other's presence."

I was still marveling at how soft Aunt Mastoureh seemed to be, helping Mother with the meal in a quiet, almost hauntingly serene manner. I asked myself, "Could the revolution have mellowed her?"

At dinner, knowing my intentions to care as I could for Father, Aunt Mastoureh asked solemnly, "Shideh, what are your intentions in your visit?"

"Beyond treatment for Father, I am working at the triage centers in our hospitals here for the wounded and afflicted soldiers."

Her look, now familiar with the bold and ominous aunt who would always have us walking on eggshells in her presence, blurted out, "Your talents are needed on the front lines for our injured and martyred Basij forces."

Mother, almost spitting out her dinner, roared back, "Shideh came back to bring needed life here, not to end her own."

It was just like old times…Aunt Mastoureh is about to detonate an emotional bomb, and Mother defuses it.

What was most curious about this moment was Aunt Mastoureh's reticent acceptance of Mother's reprimand. She exhibited a noticeable fatigue in that moment that reminded me of my meeting with Mahin. Both my sister and my aunt were still resolute in their 'revolutionary' fervor, but knowing both as well as I do, I could sense the tiring of the passion that used to be as biting as a pit bull's clench.

The requisite sigh of relief upon Aunt Mastoureh's departure seemed to allow Mother to be relaxed and conversational.

"Father is sleeping soundly now, but I have to tell you, Shideh, you gave him a necessary spark, and me as well…it is good you and Mahin saw each other."

"You know we saw each other?"

"Yes, she told us when she visited recently."

"She visited recently. She was here in Tehran?"

"Yes, Shideh, she was here; you know things are different, and we must accept her as she is. Didn't you notice the difference in your aunt Mastoureh? She, unbelievably, is more tolerant of my political moderation. I can only assume since the murder of two of her friends, Manijeh and Amineh, it has hit home how off-track the revolution has gone."

"I remembered those girls from childhood and as teenage girls joining in the demonstrations against the Shah. Ironically, they were the first women we knew who called themselves 'revolutionaries'. They joined MEK *Mojahedin-e-Khalq,* and those who did were just as responsible, if not more so, than anyone, for the overthrow of the Shah. Now, the regime has savagely executed them as well, 'the revolutionaries!' I believe there was a time when Aunt Mastoureh feared for her life as well…"

"Who executed them?"

"Oh, Shideh, the authorities, the regime, the barbarian judge; Sadegh Khalkhali—we call him Satin Khalkhali. He shows no mercy for humanity; he even had the former Minister of Education, a woman by the name of Parsa, executed in cold blood. She was a friend of Beheshti…it all makes no sense…and then Beheshti himself was killed. Violence has been the glaze of our days."

"I speak to you like this in silence. For it is now like what Grandfather Rasool used to always say, *Divar moosh dare va moosh ham goosh dare.* The walls have mice, and the mice have ears."

"You are here; your father can rest peacefully now that he has seen you. Help with the injured and the sick, but you cannot stay…this country offers little for you as a woman especially. The young men are being killed in this horrible war, and the older men are depressed and impotent and take it out on their wives. You must take your Iranian blood, heritage, and history and plant it somewhere else. America may not be the answer, but right now, our beloved country is no answer for the meaning of life. I, at night, every night, dream of Esteri often. I can see only her essence, never her face, but I wake up knowing she is with us still. Wherever you are, Shideh, I know you, too, are with us. Every hour you breathe, I only know you to have given to others."

There was so much to process. It was very hard to sleep that night. I longed to speak with Richard, but that would not be possible at this time.

Chapter 38
In the Company Philadelphia,
Pa. Fall, 1984

With Harold back from his training, Richard and he decided to meet up at Kelly's on 'The Main Line', a stone's throw from the Villanova campus for old-time's sake. The place was not the sentimental, crusty dive bar. It was back just half a dozen years before; it now had the look of every derivation of TGIFriday's.

"Well, Blaze, before I tell you about my cool new apartment in Maryland, it's for real—I'm an official graduate of the farm. Even better, my station is going to be where I was told I would be, unlike a last-minute switch that happened to two guys I was with at the farm."

"What do you mean…what happened to them?"

"They got assigned to not only two different countries than they assumed they would be stationed at but also what their pre-training at the Langley was directing them to."

"Crap! That sounds harsh."

"Not as harsh as my roommate down there, who got washed out with three days to go."

"Washed out?"

"Yeah, the dude was an older Air Force guy in his mid-thirties. The guy actually flew in 'Operation Frequent Wind' in the waning days of Saigon. Got thousands of Vietnamese out…I thought he was a stud, ripped, disciplined…I don't know. I suppose maybe he worked in the civilian life for too long."

"But wouldn't that add to his cover?"

"Blaze, that's what I thought, plus what he did back in Nam—shit, that should qualify him alone in my book—not to mention he has a wife and three kids and all. I loved the guy; you would, too."

"So, is he out, out?"

"No, I guess the deal is you have the option to be in the 'White Division' as an analyst, accountant, or gopher. Not for me…if I wash out, I wash out."

"You mean not for the United States."

"Wait, sorry, I'm talking about myself. I just have no one else I can talk to about this shit. I wanted to tell you about the training and all, but how's the banking world and all, your girl?"

"Well, I'm glad you have a little time to talk before this place packs up with people. Yeah, it looks like I could be going from almost taking the job in Florida to serving the old USA in some way. I put in my papers, I'm out of the bank, and I have been going through the process for the company with the D.O.D., the references and all."

Pressing his beer mug tightly, Harold just let out his signature laugh.

"Blaze, you're joking!?"

"No, do your tradecraft nonsense…check me out…I'm going in if it all works out."

"H-O-L-Y shit! Just like old times, I…I…Blaze, just when I have all this crap to tell you, you outdo me. What does your uncle Ryan say about this?"

"He hasn't heard about it yet. He still thinks I'm with the bank. I always felt he didn't think I had the stuff you have, Harold. I have something to prove to him."

"Blaze, if you don't, my saying so if you're really getting in, you can't have anything to prove to anybody outside the organization, really, that's a definite. Does your girl Shideh know?"

"Well, this came about after her big thing went down."

"What is her big thing?"

"Harold, I don't know if we broke up, I don't know if we are a thing, I really don't know, but in a nutshell, she went back to Iran. She wants to help with her ailing father and nurse the soldiers who are being massacred from the Iraqi invasion."

"Wait…For real? Okay, let me get this straight: your girl went back to Iran, and you are in the process of trying to get into some intelligence service, maybe even the C.I.A., the United States C.I.A., mind you! No, no, no, this does not make sense. Blaze, if you cannot level with me, is there something going on? Are you already in and working on some OP?"

"Harold, no, it's simple as that…"

"Blaze, nothing that's simple! Those motherfuckers just bombed the shit out of our embassy in West Beirut, killing sixty-three and eight of my C.I.A. brothers and sisters."

"Harold, who are those 'motherfuckers?' Anybody just reading a newspaper knows it was Hezbollah…what's your point?"

"Blaze, Hezbollah is Iranian-backed. I mean, does the D.O.D. know? Does anyone know your girl is an Iranian? Who just started working her first job out of college at a prestigious hospital, and now all of a sudden is back in Iran…you will, in some part of the process, if you haven't been through that yet, be asked if you are related or familiar with any foreign nationals!"

"Harold, I've thought all that out, but it's Shideh. For crying out loud, she is like the purest person either of us has ever known."

"Blaze, we know that, but the optics, you know the optics of this relationship, for either of you—just the sheer expediency of it all. Crap, I thought I was part of a lot of action with the subterfuge drills in OPFAM and the sleep deprivation and all that. However, you have had a hell of a lot of stuff going on. I don't know, have I had too many beers, or is it you?"

"I just want to contribute, make a difference, not exist somewhere at some obscure Florida bank. Shideh is bandaging amputees in her country; women in my bank who eat two jelly donuts and drink three coffees before they help customers surround me. I was really pissed as well when I saw that about the Beirut bombing. As far as Shideh is concerned, I think about her constantly, but I'm not even sure if I'll ever see her again."

"Blaze, I got to tell you…it might be either the worst thing or the best thing if you never see her again. You know what I feel about her and you both, but right now, when you hear a rumor, it is oftentimes valid, but when you hear a rumor from the intelligence community, well, that hearsay has greater validity. The hearsay is that there is some real crazed shit going on with the nation that calls us 'the Great Satan' and us. The Mideast to me, well, Western Africa seems like Heaven on Earth compared to there, and Iran is some complex place!"

"Well, you, me, we are in the intelligence community, and we don't merit hearsay."

"Blaze, let me tell you what I wanted to tell you about—my really cool apartment. I won't be seeing either you or it for a while. I should just describe it."

Chapter 39
Who Is the Foe?

Prior to my arrival back in Tehran, I had read and heard from Iranian friends the horror of the *defa-e-moqaddas,* the sacred defense of our homeland. The dismembered boys who had lived and the wailing of the grieving mothers whose sons had not made both hospitals and the city a nightmare you never woke up from. The truth of those stories before, during, and after my witnessing of the carnage was real. The stories I had heard of the actions of the *Komiteh-ha-ye Enghelab* or Revolutionary Committees seemed almost apocryphal. I was soon going to know just how real, nefarious, and confused the *Komiteh* actually was.

Working as a scrub nurse with me was a beautiful Iranian-Canadian girl named Friya Hannoum. We had developed a kinship for the past few weeks as she left her job at Mount Saint Joseph Hospital in Vancouver, B.C., to do the same work I had taken up. She regaled me with stories of Vancouver, 'A Sea like the Caspian, mountains like the Alborz, every ethnicity like Tehran'. She loved to tell me about the city, her country, her days in the rigorous nursing program at The University of British Columbia, but she often changed the subject when I asked her about her family. I was only to find out years later that her parents had left in 1979, leaving everything behind. She told me her father was in the Imperial Guard and had fled with relatives to London. From there, her family immigrated to Burnaby, Canada, and opened up a cigarette store, which later became a convenience store and, ultimately, one of the most successful chains of convenience stores in the provinces. In between our frustrations of not knowing if we were making a difference, we spoke little about politics but much about men. I told her about Richard.

On a particularly chilly day, Friya and I had gone into the hospital at four o'clock in the morning and left at seven o'clock at night. Leaving the hospital, we waved goodbye to one of the doctors and hailed a taxi for the very short drive to my house. Friya had agreed to eat Mother's dinner of *Kuku Sabzi*. I spoke to Mother before leaving the hospital, and she gleefully told me how she had made one of her rare solo excursions to market, just to get the freshest of herbs and spices to make this meal well.

Before we even entered the taxi, three men, all dressed in untucked black shirts, called us out. I knew this was trouble when I heard one man, with a belly protruding to the body of the car, refer to us as *gheir-khodi* or outsiders.

"Come here. Were you about to travel with the man you waved to?" The thin, pocked-faced man shouted. My thoughts were to follow Mother's advice quickly; stay modest and stay quiet. I knew both Friya and I were wearing *Roopooshes* that were long and ugly enough to meet 'revolutionary approval'. We were dressed appropriately and modestly, and despite the indignity, I would stay quiet.

Choosing to speak yet answering respectfully, Friya claimed, "We are going home."

"You are sisters?" The over-bellied one queried.

"No," Friya said right back, "we are hospital workers, comrades, working for the patriotic soldiers, the revolution, and the sacred cause."

The third one, silent to this time, spewed out, "Oh, you are American?"

"No," Friya answered, "Canadian."

"Kafir—nonbeliever. Just the same, and you, the quiet one, are you Canadian as well?"

"No, Iranian."

"But your accent does not tell us you are Iranian. Show us your identifications."

Friya pulled out hers, but as chance would have it, I had left mine at home in my haste to get to the hospital in the early hours of the morning.

Before I could offer an explanation, we were both pushed inside a van and driven to a Ministry of Intelligence office. While the three men stunk of sweat and cigarette smoke, the ministry office was surprisingly immaculately clean. Immediately, this made me believe we would be released, our apologies delivered, and our appreciation for our hours of work for our countrymen shown. Four hours of interrogation later, with just a glass of water and no food, I had visions of landing in the hellish Evin Prison. Friya was across the large, brightly lit room, safe but looking terrified.

The questions were endless and inane. In between stuffing their mouths with bites of *Halvah* and cigarette butts, they would ask, "Why are you both really in Iran? What do you get from this? Will you stay in your motherland? What friends in your countries do you still communicate with? Do you stand with the revolution?"

My favorite one was 'Repeat your names and dates of birth'. We were hurled an incessant amount of insults *monafeqin*—hypocrites, 'Western apostates', etc. My mind roamed back and forth to our cleansing and bandaging wounds of the dozens and dozens of young boys coming into our care, to these misfits who represented the 'revolutionary society' that was supposed to exist. Who really was the *monafeqin*?

A younger, distinguished-looking man came into the room. He appeared more Italian than Mideastern, but perhaps I was just exhausted. At first, he seemed inured to the cacophony of his slovenly *Komiteh* associates, not even looking up at their endless gibberish. He had been shuffling papers on the other side of a large desk as if he were in a room alone with bad T.V. on in the background. When I repeated my name for what seemed like the one-hundredth time, popping his head up, he called to me, "Did you say Shideh Ghasemi?"

"Yes…I have been saying it all night."

"Are you a relation to *Seyedeh Mahin Ghasemi?*"

"Seyedeh? If you mean 'Mahin Ghasemi', she is my older sister."

The youngish man, in a scene that could only be described as 'pulling rank', called to the three cigarette-smoking men. Initially, they seemed to ignore him. In a demonstrative gesture, he called them into the outer room. I could only hear curses spewing back and forth between the four men. Finally, the youngish man came out, offering a tray of *Halvah*, which his three partners had been consuming ravenously throughout our interrogations. The three men in black disappeared mysteriously and (I'll call him Arash) apologized profusely. He told us we had a ride with an escort to our homes.

His apologies came one after another. The 'security escorts', dressed more polished, were waiting for us. The engine of the jeep we were being driven by drowned out Arash's pleas for forgiveness. As we were led away, we could vaguely hear something about the 'hero of Lebanon'.

Other than Friya intimating that we should still stay together, we said nothing in the vehicle ride home. Upon our arrival home, two of the security escorts jumped out of their side, nodding, in a puzzling show of deference, to each of us.

Opening the door, Mother, as expected, was sobbing with Father, who, in a show of strength, had gotten himself up, consoling Mother all night.

We both devoured the *Kuba Sabzi*. Surprisingly, but not shockingly, Mother offered Esteri's room for Friya to sleep in. The room had been unoccupied since Esteri's death. I had not yet told Friya of either of my sisters. We embraced, sighing at the end of a long, tiresome, and frightening day. Friya said softly, "Tomorrow, please tell me the story of both of your sisters."

Chapter 40
Mexico City

'Patience, Persistence, confidence'. Those were the last words of advice about the process of getting into the 'company' that Harold gave Richard. The confidence aspect he needed the most was for giving the news to his mother about the career move. She knew he felt his talents were not being met at the bank, so he decided to lead with that. Much to his amazement, she was happy when he told her that he would be using his finance skills in a job with Lockheed, which was actually his cover company. He could not yet tell her he was actually working for the C.I.A., but he did say that the job required some international travel. To his surprise, she brought up Shideh and asked if 'International travel had anything to do with the Mid-East, the direction of Shideh?'

Richard's answer, of course, was true, "Absolutely not." Her question made him ponder if his mother was actually thinking about what he was really getting himself into.

After a month's training at Langley and barely surviving the farm, Richard was finally handed his field assignment. He got himself an apartment in Falls Church, where he spent a total of ten days before he was off to his assignment as a case officer in Mexico City. Having been an Honors student in Spanish back at Northern Catholic, Spanish seemed to come back easily to him in his immersion course. After his training at headquarters and the farm, Richard felt he was an incubator of field knowledge; however, he was soon going to find out how little he knew and how much he could really learn. His training in COMINT, or Communications Intelligence, and ELINT, Electronic Intelligence, would be taken to another level with his OTS officer, Jim McKeever, in Mexico City. McKeever was an old-school agency veteran out of Boston and a Holy Cross College graduate. Despite his rough exterior, his heart and his mind were thicker than his Bostonian accent. Richard's whole education on how the agency, politics, and the world work quickly advanced around him. He was the 'Rube', as McKeever, the 'Vet', loved to call him—sheer chemistry right from the start.

"So, yeah, Holmes! Well, I know what the agency call name for you is—'Flash', so basic, so primal—well, around here you'll be the 'Rube',—the station chief doesn't even have to refer to you as that, but I will, and just call me VET, because that's what and who I am."

"I'm down with that."

"Good. So I know pretty much about you: Jersey boy, college boy, high IQ, competitive athlete at one time, Uncle was in F.B.I., you played nice with his private agency, your buddy, also in the agency now, was the star, you wanted out, worked for a bank, you are organized, your father is deceased, two sisters, and a mystery girlfriend. But in time, you'll tell me why she is a mystery. Did I get it down pretty right?"

"Yeah, except the 'mystery girlfriend' part. I didn't know my girlfriend was a 'mystery'."

"Well, obviously, you know, I got that stuff from an agency cable, and the agency which knows everything, decided to, in their way, identify her as that. They did that by just putting 'foreign girlfriend'."

"Wow, I guess you got me down pat."

"Rube, nobody knows anybody, 'down pat', remember, that's surface stuff. Stuff I could find out from a polygraph. But I tell you one thing, the fact you were placed here with me, with our station chief means you are at the highest level of trust in the agency; apparently, you are AWT."

"What's AWT?"

"That's what we old guys in the agency refer to as someone who 'Angleton Would Trust', yes, before you ask, I worked under him, and look what the agency did to that old bastard. And someday, I bet he will be hailed as an agency hero, proven right about the moles in the agency. You'll learn that 97% of the people who come into the agency do it for the right reasons, and the other 3% are politicians, incompetents, or traitors; you'll figure it out. Your eyes and your rep tell me who you are; now I'll cue you up with your competency. I worked with some of the greatest this agency ever knew—Gust Avrakotos, Antonio Mendez, and Josh Levine."

"I'm hearing about Avrakotos, and everyone knows about Mendez, but who is Josh Levine?"

"He was in the Mideast with us as well, but as an NOC—Non-officially classified. One of the most effective NOCs, so I would and could never tell you or anybody. He was the one who saw the Shah's dissension years before the Shah saw it. Hell, Carter was still kissing the Shah's ass years after Josh saw the Shah's fucking fragility. Not that, that, was brain science as 'Peanuts', that's what we called Carter. He knew nothing about what his own Ambassador, Bill Sullivan, was doing with Khomeni's man Bazargan. Sully was negotiating a back-channel deal with those bastards in Iran, an island of stability. Remember that speech? We were peeing in our pants when we saw that; well, now we got Ronnie. The jury is out on him, but at least he appears stronger to the globe."

"So, you were in Iran?" Richard asked curiously.

"Oh yeah, but I was first in Greece with Gust; he's my all-time best. If you learn an ounce of what I learned from 'Dr. Dirty', you will be a stud around here. I hope I'm back with him someday—he's shaking it up in Afghanistan; he's amazing, he got a congressman to lobby and get millions of more budget dollars to help get guns to the *mujahideen.* You know he's a hero to so many of us, not so much for all the incredible things he did in the field, but how he told the head of the Euro Division to 'go fuck himself'."

"Really?"

"Twice. They wouldn't give him the Helsinki position…nobody deserved it more. He even learned the language backward and forwards, but he wasn't their waspy pretty boy."

"How about Iran?"

"I'll tell you four things for now about Iran, and then we got to get to work. We've been chewing it up too long.

1- ***We hated the Shah***-He was a little, pompous prick. Even Henry Precht over at State hated him.
2- ***We loved the Queen***-She should have run the country. She was for real and everybody loved her. She was helping poor children in the hospitals and the literacy centers while Shah was fucking the pride of Persia.

3- ***We had Khomeini's telephone lines in France bugged***-And even with all we knew what was coming, hell, nobody in Washington wanted to help the Shah. Carter was clueless, and everybody purposely kept Carter clueless.

4- ***Iranians trust foreigners less than Argentinians trust foreigners***."

"Let's get to work tradecraft, let's talk tradecraft."

The light from the skylight was fading on the linoleum, and my first hour in Mexico City was more educational than any hour I had ever spent in my life.

Chapter 41
Friya

I woke up early despite the nerve-racking night. Sensing Friya was awake; I peeked into Esteri's room only to hear her utter, "*Che khabar?* What's new?" Laughing viscerally, we both got up and headed to the courtyard. The courtyard and garden, impeccably manicured and cared for by Mother, were always a place of peace for us. It was painful to watch how much trouble Father had just moved to his favorite spot.

This morning, coming of his own volition, Father joined us for the tea I had heated and the cut-up oranges pulled from our tree. Friya and I were exchanging stories about our families. Father joined in, listening intently. Friya also had two sisters, one older and one younger. One sister lived in Switzerland, and her younger sister, Shirin, lived back home in Burnaby. The more I was around Friya, the more animated she would get. Her stories about her family and her school days in British Columbia were worthy of a novel. Father added to the conversation, "I am happy that my daughter has such a good and loyal friend. I only regret three things in my life. One that we could have had a better vision of what was to come with this revolution; two, that I had visited Ahmad Abad, the home of the great Mossadegh; and three, I live to see that my daughter finds a man who will plant the rose of love in her heart." Friya had tears in her eyes at Father's paraphrasing of Omar Khayyam's words. Although Father's health was declining, his mind was not. His mood, of course, was sentimental yet sanguine. It was time for us to get back to the hospital.

Late that afternoon, we stopped for a break after several hours of healing the most stomach-churning wounds on the heads and bodies of our young boys. Saddam Hussein was now using chemical bombs from his diabolical western supported war chest. Nothing made sense that an Islamic country would do this to another Islamic country or any country with living beings. One would think that the 'Death to America' and 'The Great Satan' images embossed on American flags along Dr. Fatemi Street, Taleqani Street, Tohid Turnpike, and all the other roadways in and out of Tehran should be replaced with slogans of hate and venom to Hussein. Friya blurts out that thought while working at an operating table trying to save the leg of a rail-thinnish sixteen-year-old boy soldier, his body glazed with patches of oozing particles of the monstrosity of war. Perhaps from the fatigue of both the hours and the sights, Friya was louder than she should have been.

As we walked outside, several women were gathered, exhaling the efforts of what we all were trying to do.

One woman, walking in our direction, offering no hello or a good afternoon, today, with darts in her eyes, exploded to Friya.

"Did you have words to defame the revolution?"

"*Bebabakhshid,* are you speaking to me?" Friya returned in her most delicate of chosen words.

"Yes, I'm speaking to you. Are you questioning the revolution, our cause, and our enemies?"

At this, Friya could not remain silent. Pointing to the emaciated bodies of horror, "I'm questioning this, as you should, not some mere dishonest distraction of what we face every day!"

Aside from the moans of pain, there was silence and a palpable pause in everyone's activity. No one spoke, and the arrival of more wounded soldiers to treat broke the immediate tension with more obligatory tension.

Friya's honesty could not be thwarted, a deep clear life of strength radiating from a face of innocence. We were drawn together by this, and I loved her for it. I did remember Mother's advice, however, and the 'mice in the walls' need not hear her words of truth as all around felt it. She stood in that moment like a shrine with a voice of hope.

Chapter 42
The Plate

Richard saw more action and learned more field-craft in his first few months than he could have ever imagined. Jimmy Mac, a term he would never call him in person, taught him so much and saved his backside, literally and figuratively. They were running OPS, dragging down major cartel connections. Reagan lifted the ban on C.I.A. wiretapping, and 'the Vet's' tech machinations allowed them to place taps on every consequential Mexico City politician, their connections, their mistresses, and their grandparents, all in the agency's ear. They fed incredible Intel to their partners in the DEA and relished in the successes of American hero Special Agent 'Kiki' Camarena's busts. They were helping him get close to 'El Jefe', the boss of all bosses in the cartels, Miquel Angel Felix Gallardo.

They didn't do too badly out in the field, either. In his first field OP, in a meetup with 'drug couriers' from Guadalajara, 'Vet' saved Richard's 'ass', as he would say, and the life of another experienced DEA agent. They had the whole sting set up minus one small issue. The jeep Richard had rented out of Texas still had its Texas license plate on it. Richard had forgotten a small but huge detail of changing the license plate from a fake Texas plate to a fake 'Distrito Mexico' one. They were instantly 'made'. Three cartel vehicles on a dead-end street surrounded a DEA agent, Eugenio Moncardo and Richard. Their backups did not immediately arrive. Richard figured the best scenario would be that if he were to be wounded, he would shoot himself rather than be alive while being beheaded. Before he shuttered another thought, there was a massive explosion, sending the three makeshift cartel pickup trucks into the air. Out of the corner building came the 'Vet' himself, shooting to kill three of the nine cartel hitmen disguised as drug runners. The others burned outside their vehicles. The diethyl in their bricks of cocaine incinerated their cars, landing both bodies and vehicles looking like a bizarre scene of crusted snow. It turned out that the Vet had gone ahead and planted explosives on the cartel member's vehicle. 'Easy to do—I didn't bring thousands of dollars of cash to the El Sequero brothel last night; I brought it to pay some kids to go under the cars of those bastards'. Having that done, he followed Richard and Moncardo in what he called a 'supervisory capacity', with the detonator in his pocket.

Musing to himself, heading back to the station, "I'm thousands of miles from our Jersey tomato garden in body and mind," Richard understood the war zone he was in. The Vet never let him forget it. He called it the escapade of the 'Plate'.

He told him, "Every OP going forward, remember that fucking plate…never forget the minutiae, whatever you do…think plate."

Several weeks after the 'plate' escapade, a cable came in from headquarters. McKeever, his deep brows wrinkling in a queried look, read it. Astonished, he read it again. Looking at Richard, reading it, looking at it, finally saying, "Rube, the station chief is going to ask the same question: do you have any idea why you are being asked to see the DCI?"

"Director Casey?"

"No, the 'Wizard of Oz'…who the fuck do you think I am talking about, and don't give me that look, I'm writing up stellar reports…the plate is our secret?"

Richard had to tell him about his non-relationship, 'relationship' with William Casey.

"My dad and Director Casey were old friends from Fordham. When I was a kid, we had to go along with my parents to events I always remember as being boring. He came to my dad's funeral; I think he had been the SEC chairperson or something. He told me something about being my 'dad's man'. Never even thought of him all these years, truthfully."

With a rueful look, the 'Vet' said, "No kidding…the Rube and the director…I hear he's quite a character, shaking things up for the better in this company for sure."

"My dad and my uncle always did say that he looked like a feeble farmer, but he was the smartest guy in the room, in any room, at all times."

"That's Casey…well, remember us small people on your way up."

"Vet, I'm sure it's something about family. He wants to help institute a scholarship in my dad's name or something. My mom has been talking about that for years; we'll see."

"Well, you'll see. Just remember to lean over when he speaks; he sort of mumbles."

"I do remember that, and I do remember my uncle saying, 'Casey mumbles with purpose'."

Chapter 43
Death of a Parent

The death of a parent is an awakening of sorts. The stages of life are relived through the memory of time spent with them. Most of all, it is the security that they had provided through the contours of comfort, conversation, and, yes, even control. Father died in his sleep, a husband, a Father, a mathematics teacher who lived and breathed what to him was the genuine reality of his heroes' spiritual lives, Mohammed Mossadegh and the poet Omar Khayyam. It was fitting that Mother found him lying, with his book of Khayyam perched on his chest, in final rest. Before his final rest, he had muttered simply, "Thank you, my rose."

Since there was no information of Mahin's whereabouts and how to communicate with her, Mother would be grieving twice, both for the loss of her husband and the inability to have her eldest daughter grieve with her. The darkness of my return to my homeland was now all too unbearable.

My conversations with Richard were never but a few moments. His voice would come in and out among muffled sounds. I was always unsure if it was the mere distance or if the regime was listening in to my calls to America. It was perhaps better if we spoke briefly. As Mother and I washed Father's body before placing the white sheet around him, she looked up at me in a curious manner.

Holding back her tears, she said sternly, "Shideh, you must now begin the rest of your life."

I understood what that meant. After the third day of mourning, I was able to connect with Richard and tell him of our sadness. I heard Richard crying on the other end. It was enough for me to hear, to feel once again before we were cut off all too soon. The impossibility of our relationship seemed more often, just that, ridiculously impossible. There was something in his feelings that despite the war zone I was in, the darkness that surrounded me every day, the distance of our cultures, the distance of our language, the distance of our geography, the distance of our time zones, there existed no distance at all.

Friya had been with me throughout the first nine days of our mourning. After that, I did not hear from her. She had not appeared at the hospital. All my attempts to contact her were unsuccessful. Our nursing supervisor could only tell me one day, "She went back to her home in Canada." I felt pained by the notion that she would not communicate a goodbye to me. Although strange, I knew the gloom that embraced my being and the nineteen pounds that I had lost was perhaps manifested in different ways with other people. I accepted, and she went home on her own accord. I would, however, resolve to be with her again.

Chapter 44
Meeting the Director Unexpectedly

Langley, Virginia 1985

Two young men, wearing polo shirts, looking like boys out of Hollywood central casting, greeted Richard, landing into Dulles. The two men escorted Richard right into a waiting, black, four-door Oldsmobile Cutlass Supreme. Richard commented on how he 'never saw a four-door Cutlass'.

"Special makeup for the company," the freckled face bespectacled, beige shirt-wearing one responded.

Arriving at the Virginia Route 123 entrance to the agency, Richard recalled not even knowing about that entrance; he always used the George Washington Parkway entrance. Arriving through security gates, the men parked right in front of the Nathan Hale entrance, as it is known. Richard and the men were greeted by two additional maître de-looking middle-aged men who escorted him up to the seventh floor. Although he spent several months in his initial training here in Langley, he never had been up to the seventh floor. Richard now felt like he was in an unknown universe.

Getting off the elevator for the seventh floor, Casey's secretary, Betty Murphy, greeted him immediately. "The director is expecting you."

Walking into the office, before he could even scant an eye on the mythical figure resembling a cartoon character, he noticed the chaotic assault of papers on Casey's desk. Still not knowing why he was summoned, he would tell himself, "The desk belies the brilliance of the man." The man's mind was sharper than his surroundings, to say the least.

The conversation was the most decipherable of Casey's voice Richard had heard that afternoon.

"Richard, you look like the spitting image of your dad, Ted, on our days at Rose Hill."

Casey began to recall stories of his father at Fordham that Richard had never known. "We once had this stern Jebbie professor for Physics. One day, the professor was late, and your father donned the professor's academic robe he always left on his desk chair. He starts imitating the professor's unintelligible writing on the chalkboard. The professor came in and leaned against the doorway, watching for what seemed like a few minutes. Realizing we weren't laughing, Ted saw the prof and turned white. After that, we never had a single better Jesuit teaching us."

Casey, navigating pencils and paperclips in his hand, went on, "I loved your mom, Ruth, and Dad. Sophia always says that they were the most loving couple we had ever known, not to mention your dad was the most honest of men I had ever met. We did a lot of social things together. You know Fordham was your dad's second love. I don't think a man did more for both the Jesuits themselves and Fordham."

"Let's get some lunch; you must be starved, crossing a time zone or two, jet lag and all."

Heading to the dining room across from his office, it seemed like the food, in great proportions, was planned and placed in front of them. As the egg salad oozed down on his chin, Casey became less discernable. He seemed to rush his food and speak largely about his pride in the agency.

"Richard, you are a part of the turnaround in this place. You know we are larger, better, more efficient than ever. We have more PhDs here per acre than anywhere else in the world. Your class had 120,000 inquiries; 500 were hired, and as you know, half of that came out of the farm, including you. The president unlocked the cuffs, the old admiral, Turner, had thought were placed on him. Richard, human Intel is still the commodity, the steak at our table; we got to use it aggressively."

With that, Casey finally sprung up. Richard, getting the cue, put down his half-eaten BLT and followed the hunched-over Casey back into his office. Casey's secretary followed them into the office and placed a file dossier on what appeared to be an available area on Casey's desk. Casey murmured, "Please look."

As Richard picked up the folder, he perused the pictures of dozens of photos of a girl, possibly Italian, possibly Mideastern, wearing a UCLA tee shirt, to photos of the same woman in a burka, two in a chador, and one where the same woman with long hair looked like a European tourist.

"Does she look familiar?"

Richard saw some familiarity in the facial eye regions but could not place her at all. There were names, apparent aliases from 'Safeer' to 'Ava Toricelli', to 'Khaleh Azadi' to 'Andrea Forte'. Casey, now conducting another conversation on a satellite phone, simultaneously writing notes on a yellow pad, biting his tie, pointed to the bottom of the file where it said 'Mahin Ghasemi'.

Richard's BLT had reached his throat.

Not knowing whether he was talking to him or the person on the phone, Richard heard Casey say, "She's the most potent female for the regime outside of Nilufar Ebtekar, the woman you know as 'Tehran Mary', the spokeswoman for the regime during the hostage crisis. But this one is not in the open; we have been tracking her for four years, and she's a ghost. We believe she orchestrated Dawud Salahuddin's, the killer, escape into Montreal and then to Europe. We have strong Intel in the way of pictures of her being the transporter of the suicide bombers in Lebanon. She was trained in summers in Lebanon while in college at UCLA under Mostafa Chamran, a renowned American professor, a brilliant guy actually, who founded the Iran and the Muslim Student's Association and went back to Iran, dying a hero in the Iraqi-Iran War."

Casey, now what seemed to be in his second conversation on the phone, announced, "She's lethal—we have to get her…one more thing, we are quite sure your friend, Shideh, knows nothing about her sister's history. Yes, her phones have been tapped extensively."

Now off the phone, Casey's notorious dandruff, more noticeably nestling on his shoulders as he leaned forward, "Richard, we need your help. We'll bring you back here to headquarters for six months…"

"Director Casey, Shideh, I mean, is she going to be alright."

"Yes, Richard, we even got her out of one of the regime's shakedowns— she was detained with another nurse by the *Komiteh*; we are taking advantage of their disorganization and their multifarious egos, we have a NOC in there, and he got them out—it could have been brutal for her. We are going to give you a special satellite phone designed by a Russian asset of ours to call her— no longer will you have the muffling sounds and be cut off after 30–40 seconds…"

"You'll work out of headquarters; Shideh is to believe you work for Lockheed, of course. You just have to inquire when the next time she will be seeing her sister, we'll train you for that. Got to go; after that, I'm putting you down in another station in Managua, got something even bigger for you…after all this, Sophia and I will have you and your mother up at Mayknoll, covertly, of course," Casey said wryly.

"Bye. Got Bud McFarlane coming in."

A nervous-looking Marinesh man came walking in; Casey grumbled in my direction, "Richard, we'll protect what you got, don't worry."

Chapter 45
Transitions

It seemed impossible to contact Friya. I worried the worst, but I was overwhelmed with my concerns about leaving Iran and getting Mother out.

It was easier than we all had assumed to get Mother to leave Iran. After Father's forty-day mourning period, *chehelom,* Mother realized there was little or no one left to love or to care for in Tehran. Her memories of northern Tehran would be tarnished with tragedy, sadness, loss, and indignity. Nearly all of her friends and relatives had relocated to Southern California, somewhere in France or the UK, specifically, London. The mere mention of moving to America was immediately negated as Mother felt the country of the 'free' had radicalized Mahin. London was the answer, and although the sun never seemed to come out, the haze of the bombings and the fog of war had made Tehran seem constantly overcast, so Mother never really complained. She seemed more comfortable than I ever expected her to be. One never knows how the mere sounds of war and loss pierce right through another human's consciousness, even if it is your flesh and blood, your mother.

My conversations with Richard were clearer. He described his new job. It sounded more exciting to him than his job at the small bank in New Jersey. There were things I was learning more and more about Richard, such as the fact of his ability to speak Spanish fluently. Richard would be visiting us in England before I went back to America to meet Mother. It seemed like I was in, again, another world. I had been cleansing war-torn wounds, working often among darkness, death, and chaos. It felt comforting finally to have the peace of Mother settling in what appeared to be a safe place.

When Richard finally made it over, Mother intimated to me that Richard had 'kind and caring eyes'.

She also said, "He must have an important job; it seems like he has much on his mind."

Mother was diligent, thirsting for knowledge but oblivious to the world order and unwanted chaos that afflicted so many. It was exciting as Richard was transferred back from Mexico City to an office outside of the capital district and had a beautiful apartment in Falls Church. We were beginning that process of getting to know each other again.

On more than one occasion, he appeared aloof and distant. One night it came to a head when he blurted out questions about Mahin.

"How come you never speak about your sister?"

"You have never asked about her; why do you seem concerned about her now?"

"I have never asked about her because you never bring her up."

"Well, she travels much, and we don't often speak. I haven't seen her since Burlington."

Without thinking, I let out too much. "Burlington? What's Burlington?"

"It's nothing. Nothing, it was just a weekend trip I took to see her before I left for Iran."

"You never told me; the only trip I knew about was when you went to see your Georgetown friends."

I did not know what to say. We were just reacquainting, and wanting everything to be all right, I just could not help myself. Richard's facial muscles were now a contortion of anger.

"I never even knew she was living in Burlington."

"She was, for a short while, but that was between jobs two and three years ago."

"So, what does she do now?"

Now, I was the one who could feel anger across my face.

"Why must we speak about my sister? Why have you not asked me about my feelings, my trauma of being in my country during a war? Why Richard, where are your feelings? I feel I know you less than when I left."

There were stark differences between Richard and myself now. I was wearing the gaunt look of the existence I had been trying to survive in. Richard now looked heavier, the look of leisure written across his face of what appeared to be a sedentary job. I knew he was no longer doing the hobby he loved—

running; I worried whether he was working the job he loved. His aloofness told me not.

We left each other that night with confusion in our minds. However, before he left, Richard, with eyes in a spiral look of wonder, thanked me for holding on to my heart necklace. I was unsure of us. However, I would never take that off.

Chapter 46
Dangerous Business

Mexico City 1985

Richard would be in Mexico City for a few weeks to complete his assignment. There was still time to get 'educated' by the 'Vet'.

"So, are you the new Deputy Director?"

"Fat chance of that…but I guess you trained me well enough; my next station is Managua."

"Managua? No, No, No! Not Managua for you, Rube."

"Okay, now who's the next 'Deputy Director', we get to choose our posts now?"

"I'm sorry, something doesn't fit—I've been in the agency for twenty-three years, and I have never heard of a case officer, for good or for bad, ever, being hailed back to headquarters to meet one-on-one with the DCI. Just what went on? Tell me it's a scholarship or something for your dad. Come to think of it, Casey would find a way to raise funds from a scholarship to divert to an intelligence OP—C'mon, remember, rule #1, no secrets with the secret keepers you work with."

"Well, the lunch looked great, but was fast…I did what you told me. I leaned in every time he spoke. I think he was carrying on five or six different conversations on two phones while he was speaking to me…he spoke a lot of my dad; there were a lot of stories I never knew, and then he told me about the Managua post."

"That's it? The station chief is mighty curious as well. It seems like wicked small shit for that kind of trip."

Richard was never going to tell him about Shideh's sister, as he was still sorting that out himself.

"Rube, all right, let's roll—we have a lot of work to do; two federal judges were kidnapped while you were on your excursion."

The Mexico City C.I.A. station was rolling. The detailed info garnered from both the tech skill and the solid assets McKeever and Richard put together were instrumental in the Policia Federal Ministerial and the DEA finding and rescuing the judges and proving a connection to their kidnappers and other major players in the cartels.

In a rare moment of downtime, McKeever one day brought up again, "Managua, just doesn't make sense, just doesn't, Rube, not only that, the immediate arrival of an updated state-of-the-art satellite phone. Now you don't have to run off with your spare change to call your girlfriend, your foreign girlfriend. Speaking of which, how are you going to pull that off? A lot of corporations in Mexico City, but is she going to believe you're working for Lockheed in Managua…or does it even matter?"

Richard finally lost it with McKeever, the 'Vet'. "I, like you, work for a fucking company, The company. I'm fluent in Spanish, thank God for that, since yours sucks, I go where they tell me to go, so go fuck off, Vet."

"You done?"

"I'm done."

"Good, give me credit for a few years in this business. I'm looking out for yah, Rube. You got a lot going for you…you're smart, you're genuine, not necessarily a good trait in this biz, by the way, but you're a freaking altah boy…since I've been around the fucking block, there are stations that you need the vipas, killas, Managua is one of them, and they are doing some weird shit down there."

"Vet, I signed on for weird shit."

"But what's going on down there is double-dealing weird shit, using our adversaries to sell arms to, to 'aid' the contras in Nicaragua…you're good, but that's stuff, the dirty stuff, quite frankly, it is for old scoots like me."

"Why's that?"

"Rube, I'm only going to say this once; I already called you an altah boy; maybe you don't like that, but it's a compliment. You'll have a life, maybe even a future, with your foreign gal…I have nobody, nothing but this. My wife left me after my first post. I can't blame her. I had two African gray parrots my neighbors took care of. I loved them. After my second post, Ruby, the older parrot, greeted me with, 'Who are you, who are you, Jack?' I don't even have my parrots to come home to anymore. This is no company for altah boys. One more real thing—the Director's visit. Well, at least you survived."

"What's that supposed to mean?"

"Well, you should know the history of this station, especially in regards to Win Scott. He was the station chief here in the sixties. He had the tapes and files on Oswald, who was spending a lot of time in both the Mexican and Cuban embassies before JFK's assassination. He was going to write a book about it all—he had the whole truth of that killing that tore the heart out of the whole country. Years later, two days before he was to meet with DCI Dick Helms, he died of a heart attack. They fucking killed him, Richard, and took his Oswald documents and tapes, everything."

It was the first time McKeever called the 'Rube' Richard.

Chapter 47
A Mother in Exile

Mother was calling from London. She requested that I spend the holiday with her. She seemed to be comfortable and had many stories; the best were the ones always about her friend, Gail, and her. I believe Gail was the first non-Persian Mother ever known. Gail was a widower as well and had been in the American publishing business and decided to move, in retirement, to England to be 'around a more literary friendly environment'. The two loved taking taxi rides around London. Mother said, "Shideh, do you know the London taxicab drivers are the best in the world? They have to drive around on a moped for a year or two to study the streets." She also had a native UK friend, Poppy, who was helping Mother with her English.

"One day, Shideh and Poppy asked me if I like blueberry. I love blueberries, as you know. Therefore, when I told her yes, she said, 'OK, I'm going to take you to the Blueberry store, and I think you will like it'. It turns out she said, 'Burberry…it is a nice raincoat. Do you know Burberry, Shideh'?"

"Yes, mother, I know Burberry. I'm glad you now know the difference."

"It seems to always drizzle around here, so much cooler than Tehran…The girls and I go out for Indian food; everyone seems to eat it around here. I just don't like how much people drink alcohol; they drink like they are fishes…"

"Mother, you've gotten so silly…"

"I just love laughing and being silly with my new friends. We talk about silly things, not as much gossip as Tehran either."

"Shideh, you know we must find Mahin; hers is a world we cannot understand, but she is my daughter; she is your sister."

"Mother, I have tried to be close to Mahin, and it seems it is just no longer possible. I no longer want to see her."

"Sush, she is your sister. We are all affected differently by what happened to Esteri."

"Mother, that is a lame excuse…Mahin went her direction, and you know it, long before the pain of Esteri's death."

"I am going to find your sister. Poppy has friends in the British government, and she says they would be willing to help."

"Help with what?"

"Help find your sister."

"Mother, please, I wouldn't do that."

"Why? She is your sister!"

"Mother, she might have been involved in things we don't want to know…people, bad people might be looking for her."

"*Eeentorri harf nazan.*"

"Mother, please don't tell me not to talk that way. When must I not tire from these mysterious visits from my older sister? Do you realize I suffer with the thought that she could end up like our dear Esteri, cousin Somaya, her friend Soraya, or Mostafa Chamran?"

"Who is this Chamran?"

"He was Mahin's teacher; she was his disciple during those summers in Lebanon, and I guess she didn't share that with you, Mother. He died in Dehlavieh fighting against the Iraqi invaders. He is turning in his grave right now on how repressive the revolutionary nation he fought for has turned out."

"Shideh, this is why we must find and embrace your sister; it is in a Mother's dream that she longs for the simplicity and liberty that I am finally living."

At that, Mother and daughter embraced, tears rolling down their eyes.

"I only hope for your dream to come true, Mother."

Chapter 48
Remember What to Live For

Bel Air, Maryland 1986

"Vet, Congratulations on your Distinguished Intelligence Medal."

"Appreciate that—so, you're probably wondering why I asked you to meet me out here at a bar in the sticks."

"For a sleuth like you, Vet, it would have to only be outside the Beltway."

"I'm going to allow you to call me Mac, and I'm refraining from calling you Rube. In a week, I'll be leaving for my new assignment in Lebanon, and I have something for you, but I wanted to catch up first. How's things at headquarters?"

"Well, truthfully, I felt safer in Mexico City surrounded by the most heinous of drug runners, corrupt politicians, and cartel kidnappers."

"Like I said, no longer am I going to call you Rube…you're starting to get it."

"Get it?"

"Richard, there are a ton of people, I told you, 97% who come into the agency for the right reasons, the way you and I did, but it's the deadly 3% that don't, and they're usually the ones not in the field."

"That's a serious claim, Vet. I mean, Mac, are you getting bitterly hardened?"

"Richard, I never told you about my brief stint in Iran—we were giving the information to headquarters about the rising venom toward the Shah being instigated by the mullahs. We more than clarified the Mullah's hypocrisy and anger about their land being given to the peasantry. They were using phony piety as a façade to bring down the Shah. Not to mention the backstabbing from our embassy, we were living up to our 'Ugly American' image for crying out loud. Instead, what comes out of D.C.? National Intelligence, in 1978, made a prediction that the Shah would stay in power for at least another ten years. It's like the bullshit the agency is giving the country about the Soviets—to every Joe in America. We are under serious threat from those guys, yet they are choking on their economy; Afghanistan did that to them—thank God for Gust, his guy Mike Vickers, Congressman Wilson, and that Texas beauty Joanne Herring."

"Mac, I don't remember you this pissed."

"I'm doubly pissed—Gust just sent a memo to Clair George, the DDO, to stop this whole Iran-Contra nonsense, and what happens, they put him out. The best and most proven guy the agency has probably ever had got put out to pasture in Central Africa."

"Geez, I'm sorry to hear that, but maybe you should now celebrate your award. Worry about yourself."

"I told you, Richard, I don't even have my parrots to celebrate with. I'm celebrating by being with you and our friendship and what I need to tell you."

It was not even happy hour yet, and the beers started flowing. McKeever's face was getting beet red, yet Richard absorbed every word he spewed.

"Maybe Casey is trying to protect you, but it's months since you were supposed to be stationed in Central America; it still doesn't fit why he told you he was sending you to Managua, and you're still here. But it's the best thing, you would be down there with that lunatic, Ollie North…I was worried kid; a lot of heads are going to roll around this."

"I have heard edgy stuff; what is the Director's role?"

"Put it this way, Casey and Reagan have one big thing in common—they are fervent anti-commies. Reagan, I just believe they prop him up sometimes to nod and smile. Casey is a highly moral man, brilliant, but sometimes highly moral men become lost in the responsibility of something, maybe something a master like him can't control. He also must maintain the illusion that the agency knows more than other organizations."

"Illusion?"

"We are intelligence collectors, first and foremost, but then, as you're seeing now, the politics get in the way. We knew of Republican campaign guys meeting with the Iranian clerics in Spain before Reagan was elected; imagine playing purposeful delay with American lives for politics!"

"You didn't answer my question, Mac, what is the Director's role in Iran-Contra?"

"Not to burst your bubble, but this crap is under his watch. It's all so deceitful to our taxpaying country. In addition, that's coming from a guy who has navigated deceit on a high level for a quarter century. Selling arms to a diabolical regime just after we helped send arms and chemicals to their adversary. You know Admiral Turner had this right, 'Khomeini doesn't compromise'. Damn, it looks as though we sure as hell do. Are we getting our guys back? They killed our agency brother, Bill Buckley, savagely…I'm going to do what I can to revenge that."

"Most of us think that Casey inherited the mess—like Kennedy with Eisenhower's Bay of Pigs debacle. The bottom-line-bad means, but the ends, stopping evil in the form of the Sandinistas, have to be the justified ends. I still think Casey was trying to protect you, that's the good news unless he was going to send you, a normal guy, fluent in Spanish…I don't know, is your girl from South America?"

With this leveling and commiserating with a man who not only saved his life but whom Richard looked at as a second Father, he could only answer, "No, Iran."

"Rich, I know you have a deep affinity for Casey, but now it all makes sense. I'm going to leave you with my final bit of advice…and I hope you'll appreciate where it comes from. Don't ever let them use someone you care for, and I know you care for her; I've always known and respected that for their agenda. Remember this: your faith, your family, your honest friends, that is what you live for; don't sacrifice that for your company, this company, or even the country."

"Wow, that sounds familiar."

"Well, I hope it does. Borders burn souls."

As they left that night, McKeever handed him a file folder. "Richard, old Win Scott wouldn't let them get the best of him. The men who worked at the Mexico City station for the past two decades have passed down what's here. One of the men found a trapped door beneath a parquet wood floorboard at the station with this and other tapes and files in it. Keep this, preserve it, and duplicate it if you can, just in case. And put those you love first."

Chapter 49
Mahin Faces Her Truth

I was starting to have recurring nightmares of waves of young boys advancing toward an enemy front, their bodies scared with visible lung tissue protruding above lesions of mustard gas-induced blisters across their stomachs. I never had these dreams while I was facing the actual residue of these crimes against humanity in person. It was over a year that I was away from such horrors, and now, I could not get away from those disturbing images. The most frightening of dreams was when Mahin stood front and center of the charging brigade of boys. Then I would awake, usually in a cold sweat, unable to sleep the rest of the night.

Death was around me in my safe universe, thousands of miles from the war, which was still being waged. The argument not to have a way to halt this madness was untenable. Richard called me to tell me about his family's friend who had passed away. He had never mentioned anything about this man but seemed to have great admiration for him. Perhaps it was because I was not over my father's death; perhaps it was because the image of the dying boys I had cared for would not leave my psyche. I explained to Richard that, at this time, I could not emotionally attend a wake or funeral. It was only a few weeks later when I saw a magazine article, that I found out who this man was.

Surrey, United Kingdom.

A call from my mother came in after 7:00 pm one night. I knew with the time difference; it was midnight her time; thus, the call must be important. She explained to me that she received a cryptic message from Mahin, 'she would like to see her and, if possible, Shideh'. She provided directions to a place in the countryside town of Shere. She would provide a driver and further locations. She also mentioned, 'Please, for the ears of Rasool'. That was something Grandfather created to say whenever it was not clear if 'the mice in the walls were listening'. You never knew who could be listening on the phone, and that became our family's code for our secret privacy during both the Shah and post-revolution years. Mother begged me to 'move mountains to come', which I vowed I would. I would tell my sister that I could no longer accept any surreptitious meetings. I needed to break free of the tyranny of the phobias I brought back from Iran.

I was never as proud of Mother as when she explained to me, "While she loves her new and old friends, there are certain sacred things that must be kept to oneself." We both laughed when she described her British friend, Poppy, as sporting a stunning resemblance to 'Lady Maharat Khan', a character from My Uncle Napoleon. I don't think Mother ever read the novel, but fondly, we recalled the memory of our family, Esteri, Mahin, myself, Mother, Father, and often Grandfather and Grandmother watching the show on T.V. together when I was a teenager. It was an indelible memory of unity. Mother even recalled the night Aunt Mastoureh was over, and 'she too was laughing ebulliently'. Mother couldn't resist the speculation that her dear friend, Poppy, was 'an agent of the police', as the genteel woman was far too inquisitive about both her daughter's whereabouts. Perhaps this would be innate paranoia due to the society we had lived in for many years. Or maybe it was a 'Mother's instinct', but ironically, we did find out years later that she was an agent of MI6.

If there were to be a reckoning of some life Mahin was living, a life that she was leading far different from the one she had planned, it would be Mother to look her in the eyes and tell her to change or face the consequences. Mother detested the notion that some foreign agent or some government, foreign in either distance or ideology, would once again interfere with her family, her culture, and her very life. For she had already lost a daughter, a niece, and the will to live of a husband due to the screaming hatred of someone else's passion to inflict his or her way on others. Most surprising was Mother's insightfulness and craft in giving Poppy misinformation that Mahin had contacted her and that 'she was in South America'.

It was not easy for me to get time off from work so suddenly, but since it was 'family-related', my supervisor was more than accommodating. After a long flight, I met Mother at her flat in London. Our driver, a quiet but friendly, handsome man, took us in the direction of Surrey. The English countryside was stunning. The villages, with their little flower boxes adorning every house and edifice, were picturesque. It seemed that every blade of grass was in place. We dropped off in front of a cobblestone walkway of a manor house. Out came Mahin, loosening her chador, exposing a hint of gray. Life was raging even to my all too energetic, sister Mahin. Soon, we were walking, for what seemed like hours, on a bucolic trail called the 'North Downs Way'. It was quiet, with an occasional bicyclist breezing merrily by us, uttering a friendly 'enjoy this fine day'. Mahin, in a reflective voice, described her summers in Lebanon and her desire, as she put it, to help the *mostazafeen*.

Later, we sat at a café over tea and pistachio nuts, listening to the confessions of my sister, who had given her soul to a cause, only to find out the cause was soulless. She told us about her growing disenchantment as she watched Khomeini and his minions turn against and execute his former supporters, the Tudeh party members, the MKO members, hundreds of Iranian patriots, and even a man such as General Pakravan, who had once saved Khomeini's life and prayed and often ate lunch with Khomeini in the early 1960s. She could no longer bear herself to have an iota of association with such flagrant and murderous hypocrisy, she told us. "I went with the cause to be unique in fighting for humanity, only to see this regime destroy the mere essence of humanity." The final straw for her was when word got back to her that a noted Sepah agent, a female named Arghaven Tuhgat, was placed in the very hospital where I worked, deliberately to watch and track the outside *mostakber*, oppressors, or so Friya and I <u>were</u> labeled. Mahin, sobbing at this point, informed me of the covert kidnapping of my beloved friend Friya Hannoum and her subsequent execution at the hands of the 'barbarian guards of Evin'.

Mahin, always full of surprises, to say the very least, told us the man who drove us was the very man who joined her in seeking a way out. He, a former Sepah agent as well, and Mahin had used all the resources of the guards to secretly plan their escape from the life that corrupted itself. She knew there would be consequences, and while she had safe houses in England, she planned to meet up with this man, Reza Motahhari, in Dubai in the summer. Most striking to me that day was that while Mahin and I would break down with intermittent bouts of crying, Mother shed not a tear. Rather, she was aglow in pride for her flesh and blood, who had undergone a critical epiphany.

"Mother, there will be dangerous people looking for me, and I might have to be separate from you for a long time, but hopefully, the last, long time."

"Mahin, you are never separate from me, my brave and beautiful daughter."

Chapter 50
Not Afraid of the Devil

Washington, D.C. 1987

"Holmes, the Deputy Director is on my ass. What intelligence have you been able to gather on the ghost girl, Gashemi?"

"She was in Burlington three years ago, used a funeral home and hearse as a front."

"Three years ago, are you fucking kidding me? You are as useful as a third nut on a bull."

"I'll be sure to let you know if I hear anything in the next three years."

"Holmes, that ain't gonna go over well around here—no matter how up the ass you are with the Director."

"I wouldn't be here talking to geniuses like you if I was 'up his ass'. Plus, speaking of things which 'wouldn't go well around here'—probably not a good idea to dis the Director while he's in the hospital recovering from his seizures."

"I'm telling you, you better start extracting information or make it up or something, as the guys in Berlin did in the sixties, because your head will roll if you don't, or they'll take matters into their own hands."

"Beirne, what's that supposed to mean? Pretty strong threat coming from a desk analyst."

"Suit yourself."

Richard was feeling the weight of what the Director tasked him to do. What could he do, he would ask himself? He was certainly not going to compromise what he thought he had or what he wanted to have with Shideh.

May 1987

For a place whose inhabitants were often surrounded by the gloom of death, loss, defeat, and misfortune, there was no greater a pall of gloom at

Langley than the day Director William Casey died. He had been moved to a hospital on Long Island's North Shore, close to where his estate of 'Mayknoll' was. Richard would go up to the wake with his mother and uncle and the funeral at St. Mary's Church in Roslyn Harbor, on Long Island. Earlier in December, Casey had suffered the first of several seizures while preparing to testify to Congress about his role in the Iran-Contra debacle. A few days before, he had testified before the House Foreign Affairs Committee. It was downhill from there for his health.

At the wake, Casey's wife greeted Mrs. Holmes. "Bill and I always loved you and Ted, and we wanted you to come to Mayknoll."

Turning to Richard, Mrs. Casey simply said, "You have your father's spark. Bill knew you were going to find your path, and he loved you for that."

Mrs. Casey also requested that 'rather than flowers, please send any donations to the 'William Casey Fund' for the Nicaraguan Freedom Fighters'.

The next day, with metal detectors aligning the bucolic Bryant Avenue, Richard, his uncle Ryan, and Mrs. Holmes made their way to the little St. Mary's Church. In a surreal scene, S.W.A.T. teams were nestled in the adjoining shrubbery, some on the roof of the church, some balancing telephone poles, as helicopters whirled overhead. Once inside the church, former President Nixon was in the first pew, left side. Every head of state was present, minus Vice-President George Bush. The funeral was delayed for the Bishop of the Diocese of Rockville Center, a supposed old friend of Casey. Bishop John McGann had kept the President and First Lady waiting in the basement. President Reagan and the First Lady came in, aglow in their stately splendor. They sat in the first pew to the right of Nixon, both of whom seemed to need assistance when to kneel or not.

When the bishop got up to deliver the eulogy for his 'friend', most of those in the cozy Catholic Church were aghast at the bishop as he challenged the corpse and his support of the contras. While it is not protocoled to praise the deceased, it might have been a mere courtesy to recognize the moral fabric of a fellow Christian, let alone a neighboring Catholic, who, as most knew, wherever he ventured in the world, the first two things he did, were to find the closest Catholic Church and a bookstore. The morning was saved when Jeane Kirkpatrick got up and described Casey as a 'bold, committed man, in an age rent of controversy…he was not afraid of the devil'.

As Richard, his mother, and Uncle Ryan walked out, they overheard Sophia Casey saying to a fellow mourner, "And do you think Bill is going to heaven?"

Richard wanted to jump over and say, "Of course," but was cut off by Uncle Ryan who firmly said, "I was ten seconds away during the bishop's eulogy from pushing Bill's casket out the door...what a disgraceful eulogy for a Catholic bishop in a time of grief."

Disgraceful or not, Jeane Kirkpatrick had it right, "Bill Casey was not afraid of the devil."

Chapter 51
Telling All Almost

It seemed surreal to be able to spend the holiday weekend with Mahin and Mother. Mahin expressed how she wanted to meet Richard and perhaps feel the freedoms of America once again. It seemed that she was content with recreating normalcy in her life. We all knew it would come with a price, the price of anonymity, of days and nights of looking over her shoulder, at least for the short term. We never really knew how high that price would be. We had heard of the extrajudicial killings executed by the regime in France and other parts of Europe. Nobody understood the nefarious machinations of the regime better than Mahin. Like a monstrous jilted lover at the altar, the regime left their most brutal torture and executions for those they felt had betrayed them and often their families as well. Mahin was warned of this and arranged to have us get back to London in three different cars for our safety.

During the weekend, I marveled at Mother's magnanimousness, her memory telling her not of the absence and misgivings of Mahin but rather the joys of her childhood. This was love. Only a Mother knows a child well enough if she is coming back or not. This was the love I wanted to have in my life, my future. And I envisioned Richard in that. While his mind seemed troubled as of late, his heart was always pure. With Mahin coming to terms with the truth in her life, I sought the truth as well.

Back in Maryland, Richard seemed apologetic.

"Shideh, I am sorry I troubled you with my overbearing questions."

"Richard, I want to tell you my news, my visit."

That evening, I told Richard everything that my sister told us about her life and the monumental change she is and wants to continue to go through. Richard listened the whole time without saying a word as if he were processing more than he could handle. Richard seemed more concerned about my safety and that of my mother.

"Richard, my sister has described how brutal the regime is, much more than I even witnessed when I went back to Iran. She says the Savama is no different from the Shah's SAVAK. She told me she couldn't believe that I was allowed to leave…she said, 'You must have somebody watching over you. Should I be worried for Mother and myself'?"

"I think I can speak to somebody who can help look out for you."

"Who is this someone? Oh, just someone Harold Anderson knows."

"Do you think we would be in danger?"

"Shideh, you just told me about how you had to switch cars to get to and from your sister, whom you met in the Timbuktu area of England, correct? Your sister made choices long ago; you can't just wash them away."

"Harold knows people who will look out for you and your mother. He has a good, reliable friend, but I'll tell you about that later."

Chapter 52
Needing a Purpose in All This

Richard knew that Harold had ended his tour in Angola and would naturally make his way to Casey's funeral. Out of the corner of his eye on his way out of the church, Richard recognized the tall figure lost in the crowd. He gave him 'the tap on the head signal', signifying he knew he was there. Since Mrs. Holmes came with Uncle Ryan, she would be leaving with his uncle, who was unequivocal in his anger and dismay toward the bishop's eulogy of Casey. He had no interest in driving back to Jersey to hear that ramble. Harold found Richard by his car parked off the Northern Blvd. viaduct, where earlier protestors had greeted the funeralgoers.

"I'm glad you didn't run over any of those protestors, Blaze…"

"Can't say the thought didn't cross my mind."

"Let's head up to Locust Valley. I heard of a place the Director would have lunch at every Saturday that he was on the island."

To Richard, being with Harold was a catharsis, something more than a normal old friendship would bring. It was Harold's signature sangfroid, his totally cool, relaxed nature under pressure that was always comforting. Perhaps that nature was honed in his days growing up on the streets of Baltimore, perhaps in his days as a competitive athlete, but Harold had something special; he knew it, Richard knew it, and the 'company' knew it.

"Harold, I always knew you were a hero of sorts, but you are looking great with the folks at Langley for all you helped to do in Angola, now with the cease-fire coming and all."

"Blaze, a wise man once told me, we are just intelligence collectors."

"I'm not sure he was that wise, but you guys put the Soviets and Castro's boy's backs against the wall. To say the least."

"Well, Blaze, we did do some cool stuff; my favorite OP was the 'SNEAKEROP'."

"What was that?"

"You know most of the kids had no footwear, nothing, not even a good pair of sandals. So we had 1200 pairs of sneakers from a good West Coast-based company donate them. But the best part was that they were able to affix a monitoring bug in between the EVA midsole and their signature cushioning technology. The Soviets thought they were slick using the kids to transport messages of intelligence between them and their MPLA soldiers, but we were able to monitor their every move; they never figured it out, not to mention no kids got hurt. I would say that was the perfect marriage of human Intel and technology."

"Brilliant. But how did you get that done…I mean, the sneaker part?"

"Well, let's just say the chairman and founder is not just a patriot; he's one of us."

"He's in the agency?"

"No, the man is a track dude. You know that's what I miss most—those days on the team, no brotherhood better than that."

"Amen…Yeah, we know where Belger is, but what about the other guys— I wonder where Dean Childs and Burns are? Hell—we should have gotten Nate Cooper for this. He would fake left and go right on the Russians and all those dudes. Remember, he came to school pretending he knew nothing about the track, and the brother triple jumps 51 feet for us, and we won the IC4As! But the dude I liked the most was Jim Flynn—man, he was one good dude. He could compete, and nobody would take him for a distance guy. Could party, too. You could always tell Jumbo got a big kick out of him."

"It was sure good times when I was injured and just hanging at the meets watching you guys; I got to know some of our rivals, just great guy—remember Tom Murray of UPenn? I wished I had his smooth knee lift and stride; I hear he's doing well in business. Remember the guy we called the professor from Princeton—he could fly, broke four, sure he is about to be president of the World Bank or something."

"Sorry to ramble, but your sneaker op story brought me back to all those memories. You guys did the job over in Angola."

"Yep, you might say all the damn millions of dollars the Russians sent to the leftists, were a waste…I believe that, and their Afghanistan debacle has done those motherfuckers in. I think we are going to see a completely new enemy, not a superpower like the Soviets, but a rise in global mini fundamentalist religious subversive groups. That's going to be the new battlefront. Sure saw a lot of that shit in Africa."

"I'm not sure how we got here, Harold, but I'm pretty sure we're doing good…I just don't want to end up a lonely guy like McKeever as much as I love the guy—he said 97% of us get in for the right reasons…"

"Blaze, Blaze, that's a generous number; there's some lonely motherfuckers in the company, no doubt; you heard the story about Paisley, double agent or not, murdered or not—he was one perverse dude."

"Harold, I guess you got to get out after you did something you know is consistent with the borders of your moral compass, the integrity of justice and freedom and all that…the ethos of what we are supposed to be protecting…I'm thinking some take that as a game, a joke…"

It's like Jimi said, "Many people think life is but a joke."

"Jimmy?"

"Jimi…as in Hendrix, you know, as in the greatest song ever put together—'All along the Watchtower'…damn, Blaze, how did we ever come to be you and me?"

"Crazy lucky, I guess. I have to tell you a couple of things…one is easy for me to tell, the other, well, is pretty damn difficult."

"I'm cool with both."

Richard proceeded to tell Harold about his being called in from Mexico City and meeting with the Director.

"Casey told me he was going to have me going to Managua…it never happened. My tech person in MC kept telling me there was something else…he was right…I'll get to that…but Casey created a whole new division in the agency, so secret nobody knows. You know few people know this, but he went to Fordham to become a social worker…even did a year Social Work fellowship at Catholic University…"

"The Baron?"

"Yes, plus, as an old OSS guy and an Irish guy, he had this thing for Hercules Mulligan, a hero spy of the American Revolution. Casey puts this secret division, a task force together, off the books funded by a foundation, but nobody in Congress would dare have a political problem with this. We go into troubled impoverished areas in the world, not yet warzones, and we help kids through sports and education, and if we see something bad start to develop, well, hey, we're still C.I.A. guys, well, you know, collect intelligence. It's called the Hercules Mulligan Brigade."

"That's brilliant...so you are like the Boy Scouts, the church ladies of the C.I.A.! You aren't the white ops or black ops; you're like gray ops?"

"Something like that. I think it was Casey's way of balancing, coming to terms with his sense of moral obligation to the world, instilled in him by the Jesuits, and still using our assets to fight evil and totalitarianism."

"Makes sense, only the Baron could pull that off. What's the other thing?"

Richard told him, told him everything about Shideh's sister, Mahin. Harold said he had heard about the 'ghost girl terrorist of Iran'. He told him of his concern for Shideh's and her mother's security. Harold, of course, was 'all in' on the protection of Shideh and her mother. As he put it, "If we're looking for the ghost girl, and MI6 is, you can be damn sure the IRGC and all those other regime groups that exist to assassinate are as well."

"Damn, Blaze, under our nose. One of the things I want to do before I leave this earth is to meet up again with Davoud Salahuddin. Look him straight in the eyes and ask how the hell a guy, who one day is listening to 'All Day Music' and mellow soul, can go up and shoot and kill another human being in cold blood. We had a lot in common, you know, as a brother who witnessed racism in the face growing up, but talk about directions, or was it just somebody brainwashing the brother better?"

"Ignorance...ignorance before ruthlessness. I remember reading in high school at Northern some novel about peace or something, and at the end, the narrator tells us, 'Wars are caused by ignorance in the human heart'."

"Ignorance? Ruthlessness...well, Blaze, you and I have seen a lot of that, and we are most likely going to see a lot more. I got to ask you one question, Blaze."

"Okay."

"You love that woman?"

"You know when she came back, and I heard her stories about what she did for her people, the children, I realized I had just a small idea of how special this woman is. Growing up, I had no idea about her country or her culture; they were just way over there, but there must be a reason we transcended all that was separate between us. So the answer is yes, I love Shideh. I knew all too well the pain of the loss of my dad. But Shideh lost her sister, her cousin, and her aunt, and still came to a whole new country to learn to help other people. Somebody said the Iranian women are the strongest in the world."

"Well, they have had to be; the men have been the ones who screwed up things in that culture. If you love her, you have a job and a half to explain yourself."

"Harold, that's a truth I'm worried about facing, one I can't get around. I got one for you—am I going to know about your next assignment?"

"Blaze, you better start telling me about Mexico City."

Chapter 53
Deaths Not Apologized For

We only knew that Mahin would be traveling to Dubai in the summertime. It was understood that it was best she flew out of Iran but not Tehran. Mother had received a telegram from Bandar Abbas, a port city in southern Iran, on 1st July. It simply read in English, 'for the ears of Rasool. Allah is love, and I love you. Of the moon'. That was the Farsi translation of Mahin's name.

Then it happened.

Two days later, while working a hospital shift, there was a breaking news story on a patient's television. I could hardly believe my eyes. In London, Mother saw it on her friend Gail's television, and the whole world witnessed the news that a United States Navy warship, the USS Vincennes, engaged in Iranian waters, had been shot down through a directive from the ship's captain, a civilian passenger airplane, Iranian Airlines Flight 655, killing All 290 passengers on board. The plane was flying from Bandar Abbas to Dubai in the United Arab Emirates. What I witnessed on American television was different from what Mother witnessed on London television news. The British newscast had shown videos of debris in Iran's territorial waters of the Strait of Hormuz, replete with images of human clothing; the most horrifying was the images of children's clothes. There were 66 children on board.

The American newscasters implied that the plane was aggressively flying in a pattern that would give the United States Naval military officers the impression that the plane and the speed were engaging in an act of war. The Vincennes, as the world would slowly come to learn in the following weeks, was a 'state-of-the-art' ship, nicknamed 'Robocruiser', one that would almost impossibly not have been able to contrast an onerous Airbus A300, from a smaller, svelte F14 fighter jet. Radar records showed later that the commercial plane was 'ascending' from its takeoff a few minutes away, not 'descending', which was the information the crew gave to its captain. A U.S. Naval investigation later showed that a crewmember relayed to the captain that the plane 'could be a commercial plane'. The United States claimed it was a 'grievous accident'. The world waited for an apology from the United States government. I waited to learn if it was a plane my sister was on.

Richard came to see me that night. He told me I have some very 'complex things to tell'. I reminded him that I was bred in a culture of complexity.

Mahin, he said, was on the plane. Richard had information that he gained from a picture his 'company' had possession of. The picture showed Mahin getting on the plane at Bandar Abbas. It was Mahin, although her passport said otherwise. This truth, this complexity, I was not ready for.

Several years before Esteri's funeral, many of the mourners said, *"Sham-e akharet bashe;* I hope this is your last sorrow."* How my mother could survive a second daughter perishing by means of the ignorance of others would be unbearable.

Richard told me the part of his life I did not know. His quest, he claimed, was to help others, to fight for justice and truth. He told me that the man whose funeral he had gone to the year before once said, "There are some things that are right and some things that are wrong. This life is but a trinket compared to our eternal destiny."

Unsure of my 'destiny', I told Richard I was going to Burnaby, Canada, with Mother to meet the sisters and family of my friend Friya Hannoum to establish a foundation in her name. We would mourn together the loss of our beloved sisters.

One of the items Mother had brought with her when she left Iran was a framed quote from our poet, Hafiz that Father had given Mahin on her 13th birthday.

Is it true that our destiny is to turn into light itself?
And I replied,
Dear moon,
Now that your love is maturing,
We need to sit together
Close like this more often
So I might instruct you
How to become

Mahin had started a truce with herself and God, and I pray that it is complete in eternity.

Richard knew there could be no *Marasem-e khaksepari*, or traditional burial ceremony for my sister, Mahin, and my dear friend, Friya. He did understand the importance of our time in Burnaby to work with Friya's family to honor their memories. Unannounced, Richard showed up in Burnaby, flying himself out. Mother was quietly impressed with his appearance at what was a very important time for her and me. Hours later, I was numb as he told me he resigned from the C.I.A. This was his decision, and his alone, as he explained he had 'moral conflicts ever since his meeting with Director Casey', a man he admired personally but an agency he had grown very disillusioned with.

I could now envision a future with Richard, as he had embodied the best qualities of a strength and moral compass that Father and Grandfather Rasool had lived by. He had honored his own father's wise advice to understand that your best life is to be given to your family and beliefs. As strong as those men were, it is genuinely the women in my life who have been the most caring and courageous. Even though I often could not understand nor even justify Mahin's life choices, she had been living a life guided by her convictions and principles. For this, I loved her more than one could love a sister. Mother's love was not only unconditional but enduring, as only a Mother's love could be.

Before I left for Canada, I received a telegram from Heather, my nursing preceptor, mentor, and friend when I first came to the United States. She and Erin were planning a 'memorial service' of their own for my sister and Friya in Washington when I would get back. Heather wrote in a beautiful card, 'The souls of the just belong to God'. It is from a Christian biblical verse, but it was written in the language of love and understanding that any woman worldwide would understand. The spirit of women like my mother, Mahin, Heather, and all other courageous women, I believe, will heal the soul of my native country, Iran, and the future of Iran will belong to the just.

Historical Notes

Mohammed Mosaddegh	The 35th Prime Minister of Iran, 1951–1953. Mosaddegh was a Western-educated lawyer. Charismatic, eccentric, and quirky, Mosaddegh is often described as 'the most beloved political figure in the history of modern Iran'. He was overthrown in a coup d e'tat orchestrated jointly by the C.I.A. and the British MI6 after the independent believer in a free Iran forged the nationalization of Iran's Oil industry. In *The Persian Puzzle*, Kenneth Pollack writes, 'Like JFK's among Americans, the myth of Mohammad Mosaddegh-and of the utopia he would have created had he survived in power become a fixture in Iran's political imagination'. (68). That 'myth' is strengthened in this author's mind with the iconic picture of Mosaddegh staring, as if in alignment, with the Liberty Bell in his famous visit to the United States.
Farah Pahlavi	'Shabbanou' of Iran was the wife of Mohammad Reza Pahlavi, 'The Shah'. Throughout the Shah's acrimonious rule, the Empress was always beloved for her humanitarian work and her muscular action to promote literacy centers, orphanages, educational opportunities for women and theunderprivileged, and advancement in the arts and culture. In May of 1975, The Empress received an honorary degree citation from Georgetown University. The president of the university cited her for 'her leadership role in Iranian society and culture'. www.georgetown.edu.
SAVAK	'The Shah', as William Polk writes in *Understanding Iran,* '...put his trust in fear. *Sazmanne Ettliaat va* (SAVAK), similar to the *STASI*, of East Germany. SAVAK grew 's—a wide definition who were often 's regime was, to say the least, unfortunate for ' (115) Ryszard Kapuscinski writes in the *Shah of Shahs,* 'SAVAK censored the press, books and films (it was SAVAK that banned the plays of Shakespeare and Moliere because they criticized monarchial and autocratic vices). SAVAK ruled in the universities, offices, and factories. A monstrously overgrown cephalopod, it entangled everything crept into every crack and corner. SAVAK

	numbered 60,000 agents. It also controlled three million informants, who denounced other people from such varied motives as money, self-preservation, or the desire for a job or promotion. SAVAK bought people or condemned them to torture…it defined the enemy and who should be destroyed. SAVAK answered to the Shah alone'. (46–47)
Sepah	(Army of Guardians of the Islamic Revolution). Originally established as a military branch, it contains Intelligence services, a volunteer militia called the Basij, an elite force *Revolutionary Iran*, 'In the long run, Sepah became the most important of all (Revolutionary) bodies in Iran'. (146)
Cinema Rex Tragedy-	On 19 August 1978, in the city of Abadan, Iran, four 'religious fanatics', at the intermission in the showing of *The Deer,* poured solvent in the lobby of the theater, set it ablaze, and locked the front doors. Scott Cooper writes in *The Fall of Heaven,* 'Iranians awoke to the appalling news that a single act of arson had caused the deaths of 377 men, women, and children; the final death toll reached at least 430. The inferno, the worst anywhere since the Second World War, was at the time modern history's deadliest recorded act of terrorism'. (375–376) There was blame put on both SAVAK and Revolutionary supporters for the barbaric crime. According to a *TIME* magazine article published in September of 1980, 'Iran: After the Abadan Fire', 'Alone among Shiite leaders, Ayatollah Khomeini (then still exiled) failed to condemn the Abadan atrocity'. Eventually, that same month, 'The Revolutionary Tribunal' convicted unemployed heroin addict Hossein Takbalizadeh and five others for the crime, putting them to death in public.
Iranian Airlines Flight 655	In an article published in *NEWSWEEK* on 12 July 1992, entitled 'Sea of Lies', John Barry and Roger Charles write, 'The destruction of Iran Air Flight 655 was an appalling human tragedy. It damaged America's world standing. It almost surely caused Iran to delay the release of the American hostages in Lebanon. It may also have given the mullahs a motive for revenge and provoked Teheran into playing a role in the December 1988 bombing of Pan Am 103.

	'For the Navy, it was a professional disgrace. The Navy's most expensive surface warship, designed to track and shoot down as many as 200 incoming missiles at once, had blown apart an innocent civilian airliner for its first time in combat. 'What's more, *NEWSWEEK* has learned that the Vincennes was inside Iranian Territorial waters at the time of the shoot-down clear violation of international law'.
	Iran Awakening, Nobel Peace Prize winner and accomplished lawyer Shirin Ebadi writes, 'On a summer evening in early July 1988, we turned on the television to see footage of bodies floating in the sea amid scattered airplane wreckage. Earlier that morning, a U.S. warship in the Persian Gulf had fired a heat-seeking missile at an Iranian civilian airliner, blowing it out of the sky. 'All 290 people on board perished, and it was their corpses Iranian television showed bobbing in the gulf's warm waters. President Ronald Reagan offered no convincing explanation of how the USS *Vincennes*, equipped with the most sophisticated radar gear in the Navy's arsenal, had taken the bulky Iranian airbus for a sleek, supersonic fighter plane nearly a third of its size. Few Iranians could 's captain received a medal for his performance…' (85)
Velayet-e-faqih	Literally translated as the 'Rule of the learned jurist', Khomeini adopted this, craftly utilizing it to ensure his ultimate authority in post-revolutionary Iran. In her seminal work of research, *Modern Iran,* scholar Nikki Keddie cites Islamic Theologian, philosopher, and writer Mohsen Kadivar as saying, '…neither the *Quran*, the prophet, Shi'i Tradition, nor rational inquiry supports *Velayat-e-faqih*'.

9 798889 155748